Anything For Them

(The Hunter Brothers, Book 4)

By

Lola StVil

This book is dedicated to:
Shannon Ariss
Congrats on your wedding!
Lola

Contents

Chapter 1

Jackson

It's taken months to get enough information on the terrorist cell we are about to raid. This is the best part of my job as a special agent in the FBI. We get to help stop violent crimes and save innocent lives. So imagine my fucking surprise when my boss pulls me out of the field and tells me to come see him. I watch as the FBI motorcade takes off without me.

What the fuck?!

I march into the assistant director's office and try to hold my temper as I find out what just happened.

"Serkin, why was I pulled out of the field?" I ask. He looks at me from behind his desk. He's a stout man with beady eyes and keen intelligence.

"What's going on?" I ask again.

"Take a seat," he says.

"No, I'm good," I snap.

"I said sit," he demands.

It takes everything in me, but I make myself cool off enough to sit down. There has to be a reasonable explanation. I'm one of the best they have out in the field, and if I was made to stay behind there has to be a good reason for it.

"Sorry about this, Jackson, but you are not cleared for active duty."

"Why not?"

"You haven't gone to see the staff therapist following the raid last month. You can't go on active duty until you do."

"Doctor Miller is really making a big deal about this? He usually just signs off on whatever we put in front of him and lets us go back to doing our jobs. What's the problem this time?"

"The problem is Doctor Miller is no longer on staff. He was replaced, and this new chick—I mean woman—is kind of a hard-ass."

"She won't sign off on my paperwork?"

"No, not until you actually sit down and have a session with her."

"Can't you talk her out of it? C'mon, I have better things to do than sit down on some sofa and cry about how much my mom did or didn't love me. This is bullshit!"

"Look, it's out of my hands. The other guys involved in the raid had to see this new doctor too. I'm sorry, but that's the way it goes. If you want to get back out there, you better find your ass on her sofa this afternoon."

I growl, "You can't be serious."

"Do I sound like I'm joking? Hey, this sucks for me too. I have good men I have to pull out of the field all so that Dr. Samuels can ask them about their boo-boos. But there ain't shit I can do about it. Your appointment with the doc is at 4 PM today. So, let's be grown-up here and get it done."

I can tell by the tone of his voice he's giving me an order. I also know the conversation is over as he's signaling towards the door. There is no way of getting around it. I'm going to have to talk to this Dr. Samuels. I have never met her, but I'm pretty sure this woman is going to irritate the shit out of me. I'm also pretty sure that she's one of those "play by the rules" people who has a large stick up her ass. Fuck me.

The raid last month is the last thing I want to talk about even with my family, let alone a stranger. In fact, I go out of my way to keep the events of that night buried, and now I have to dig it all up just so some hard-ass, pain-in-my-ass woman can sit there and judge me. I can't believe this shit.

I ask about Dr. Samuels around the office. When I say her name, most of the guys' eyes light up. I'm guessing by their reaction that this doctor is easy on the eyes. But I don't care if she's hot or not. I just need her to sign off on me going back to active duty. And from what the guys are telling me, there is just no way to avoid this woman.

Why can't she just sign off like the doctor before her? I can't stand people like her. Every single thing has to be done by the rules. They care more about the rules than what's right and what's wrong in this world. I have yet to meet Dr. Samuels, but I already hate her guts. So, when the time comes to see the doctor, I don't. That should let her know just how I feel about her profession.

The boss informs me that she placed yet another appointment for me. I ditch that one too. It takes a full week of me ditching my appointments for her to finally get the message. Or so I thought.

"What the hell do you mean, I have to hand in my badge?" I ask Serkin a week later.

"The doctor reported you to the higher-ups, and they are going to suspend you until you go see her."

"This is ridiculous! I don't need any therapy! You know that."

"What's so damn bad about it? Jackson, you lost two members of your team in an explosion. Maybe it's not such a bad idea to talk to someone."

"I know what I lost!" I snap so loudly that the entire office turns to look my way.

"What? Mind your damn business!" I bark at them.

"Look, I don't care how much you hate it. You have one more chance. I called her and pleaded with her to give you one more chance. You better have your ass in her office by 10 AM, or I will take your badge. Don't fuck with me on this."

It's clear now that I have no choice but to see this insufferable woman. Well, if she thinks she's gonna get me to open up, she's in for a rude awakening. She has no idea what's in store for her. She wants to meet me, fine. Let's meet.

Mia

It's 8:30 AM and my apartment is quiet. That's the first sign that something is wrong. My seven-year-old son, Aaron, has never been a fan of silence. So like any mother, I'm already suspicious.

"Aaron, what are you doing in your room?" I ask as I quickly gather the ingredients for breakfast.

"Nothing," he says.

Yeah, right.

I'm pretty sure that I need to go into his room and see what he's been up to, but since I don't see flames or hear sirens, I'm guessing whatever he's up to can't be that bad. Or so I hope. The fact is, if I don't get this food going we are going to be late. I quickly scramble some eggs for myself and make Aaron his favorite—banana pancakes with blueberries for eyes.

"Aaron, breakfast is ready," I call out.

"Um…okay."

"Come get it now, sweetie, or we will be late," I reply as I scramble to find where I left my briefcase.

"Coming!" he shouts back.

"Aaron, I won't tell you again, we can't be late. You have school, and Mommy has work."

"I know, I know."

"So, come on, mister!" I reply as I circle the living room yet again, looking for my briefcase.

"Here I am!" he says as he enters the room. It doesn't matter how many times I lay eyes on him; it still makes me smile. I can't believe he's really mine or that I made him. His wayward, curly red hair never stays in place no matter how hard I try to tame it. His bright green eyes take in the pancakes at the table and light up. His small frame and toothy grin make it hard for me not to pick him up and swing him around. He hates that. But I can't help it.

"Mom!" he groans as I scoop him up and swing him in the air. He swears he hates it, but he always giggles as I spin him. Then when I finally place him down on the floor, he composes himself and says, "Mom! Don't do that. I'm too big for that now," to remind me.

"Oh, you're right. I'm sorry. Wait, does that mean you're too big for 'happy face' pancakes?"

"No!"

"Are you sure?" I tease.

He nods enthusiastically; I ruffle his bright red hair, and he scurries off towards the plate of pancakes. I spot my briefcase in Aaron's room on the floor. I walk over and pick it up.

"Aaron, were you playing with my briefcase?"

He shakes his head "no." I walk over to the table, where my son is drowning his pancakes in syrup.

"You know better than to play with Mommy's work stuff," I remind him.

"I wasn't playing around."

"Okay, but next time leave my briefcase where I left it, okay?"

"Okay, Mom," he says as he takes his first bite. Something tells me to check my briefcase. The second I open it, a large, bright turquoise iguana leaps out. Thrown, I jump back, and the reptile flees into Aaron's room.

"Aaron, what is Mr. Henry doing in my briefcase?"

"I put him in there so you can take him to work with you. So you won't be lonely."

I laugh as my heart finally stops racing. I walk over to my son and squeeze his little face in my hands.

"Mommy's not lonely. How could I be? I've got the best kid in the world to keep me company."

"Are you sure you don't want Mr. Henry to go to work with you?"

"I think he'd be better here. That way he can protect the house. What do you think?" I ask.

"Yeah, I guess so," he says, shrugging.

"Good."

"Mom?" he calls out as he ditches the fork and eats the pancake by hand.

"Yes, honey?"

"Kevin said he's gonna bring a snake for show-and-tell, and Nancy said she's gonna bring a robot that talks. Can I bring something cool too?"

"You want to bring Mr. Henry?"

"No. Can I bring Dad?"

I didn't see that coming. It feels like someone stabbed me right in the heart. There's so much hope on his face, the thought of taking that away makes me want to cry right then and there.

"We'll see, okay? But if we can't make that happen, we have lots of fun stuff we can take to show-and-tell," I reply, trying to keep the worry and sadness out of my voice.

It's been a while since Aaron asked that his dad be present. I thought maybe he'd kind of let it go. But I was wrong. And now he wants the one thing I can't give him. He's such a good kid; he deserves a father that loves him and will show up for him. And that just isn't Tom. Every couple of weeks, he'll decide that he wants to play "father" and then he'll make plans with Aaron and won't show up.

I can't count the number of times I've watched my baby get ready for a day with his dad, only to learn that he has been stood up yet again. I finally had enough. So now, I don't share Tom's plans to come over with Aaron. I figure it's better that he be surprised that his dad is there than feel the sharp disappointment that comes from a failed outing.

I used to have daydreams about finding the right guy for both my son and me. But the fact is most men are looking for a one-night stand, or worse, they string you along until something better heads their way.

In the beginning, Tom liked playing with Aaron and doing silly things with him. But the adult part of the job was too much for Tom. He didn't like having to give up his party days and having to find a real job. He loved floating through life, getting by on his smile. And soon, it was all I could do to get him to come by and see Aaron.

My son wasn't planned, but he's still the best thing that has ever happened to me. And I won't allow anyone to hurt him, not Tom, not anyone. So, when it became clear that he would rather pretend to be a kid than raise one, I put him out of the house for good. I know I did the right thing, but in moments like this, when he aches for a father, I wonder what I could have done differently.

I push my regret and sadness aside and focus on making sure my son doesn't start his day worried about whether his father will let him down or not. I need to make him smile. I take a can of whipped cream out of the fridge and give the pancake a beard. He starts to giggle and begs for me to let him try. Soon, we are knee-deep in whipped cream, sticky syrup, and laughter.

After a quick cleanup, Aaron and I rush out of the building, just in time to get him on the bus and headed to school. I check the time on my cell, and provided everything goes well with the train, I should be at work on time. I head down to the train station and arrive just as the train is about to pull in. I think today might be a good day. But then I remember that my first patient of the day is this guy named Jackson Hunter. He's been blowing me off for over a week now, and I'm sure today will be no different. I haven't met him yet, but I already know what kind of guy he is—a grade "A" alpha jerk.

Crap, I should have stayed home with Mr. Henry.

Chapter 2

Jackson

I'd rather be doused in chum and thrown into a tank full of sharks than go inside the doctor's office. But I want to keep my badge, so I find myself in the waiting room of Dr. Samuels' office. I intend to make this as quick and painless as possible. When the guy behind the receptionist desk tells me I can enter, I nod my head and go inside.

What a fucking waste of time.

I enter the well-decorated office, where a woman stands with her back to me as she looks out the window. I don't know what the front looks like but from behind—shit! This woman has an incredible ass. I clear my throat, and she pulls herself away from the New York City skyline and turns towards me. The very second our eyes meet, the air is sucked from my lungs. I can't breathe—her beauty is literally taking my breath away.

She has a figure most men would die to get their hands on. Her dark pencil skirt is long enough to be respectable but just short enough to make a man wonder what treasures she could be hiding. There's a small split on the side that gives me a peek of her thigh. It's a cruel thing to do. A peek is not enough. My heart starts racing at the thought of my hand on her smooth, radiant thigh.

She's wearing an expensive, dark purple silk blouse that's buttoned up to the top and won't allow for a peek at her cleavage. But that doesn't stop me from noting how full and perky her breasts are. I've had my share of both real and fake breasts—so much so that I can tell what's real and what's fake even from across the room. I'd bet my life that Dr. Samuels' are one hundred percent natural. In fact, aside from a subtle shade of lipstick, everything about her is natural.

I find myself wondering about her nipples. Are they firm and plump or are they small and need to be coaxed out of their hiding place? I can make out the imprint of her lace bra just beneath the surface of her blouse. Her graceful neck and feminine jawline are just ripe for kissing. When I think about teasing her succulent, ruby colored lips, I am forced to swallow a groan. I picture what those lips could do to me, and my cock hardens.

What I find the most alluring about her isn't her spectacular figure, fiery hair, or even her delectable breasts. What has my head spinning with longing are her vivid blue-green eyes. It's as if someone stole all the colors from the beaches of Turks and Caicos and placed them in her eyes. She wears her stunning fiery copper hair in a neat bun, and has on small dark-rimmed glasses. She looks like the hottest fucking librarian I've ever seen.

In a perfect world, she'd be nibbling on the end of her glasses playfully and making suggestive remarks. However, there is nothing playful or kittenish about her demeanor. In fact, judging by her rigid posture and professional tone, she's serious as fuck. There is nothing fun or playful about her. And that just makes me want her even more.

"Agent Hunter, you decided to come see me after all," she says.

"Well, Doc, I didn't really have a choice, now did I?" I ask.

She smiles. My stomach flips. Who the fuck is this woman?

"Please, have a seat," she says as she comes towards me. She sits in the chair across from the high-end sofa. She crosses her legs, and I'm drawn to the sharpness of her heel as it dangles in the air.

"Agent Hunter, please sit down," she says.

You hate this woman, Jackson. Don't let your cock take that hate away.

"I'm glad you came by. I've been looking forward to speaking with you," she says.

"Oh yeah, why is that?"

"I've talked to everyone on your team except for you."

"Well, I'm here. What do you want to know?"

"Whatever it is you wish to tell me."

"Well, let's see. I like long walks along the beach, starry nights, and moonlit dinners by the shore. Oh, and Elizabethan poetry," I reply sarcastically.

"Agent Hunter, I know that you are forced to be here, but I truly believe this session might be beneficial to you."

"You shrinks kill me. You think you can fix me by making me talk about how I felt when my mommy took my blanket away?" She scribbles something down on the notepad beside her and then turns her attention back to me.

"Do you think you're broken?" she asks.

"What?"

"You said, 'You think you can fix me by making me talk about how I felt when my mommy took my blanket away?' My question is, do you think you're broken?"

I gaze at her. "Trust me, everything in me works...very well."

She rolls her eyes but maintains a pleasant smile. "According to your file, you have five brothers, and they are all in law enforcement. Is that correct?"

"Yeah, that's right."

"It must feel good to have family that can relate to your struggles."

"What struggles?"

"Those faced by agents the world over. It's not an easy job."

"Oh, so that's the plan to get in my head? Let me save you some time, Doc. There's nothing wrong with me. That raid was a good one, and we did what we did for the right reasons. I don't regret shit."

"You don't regret losing some of your teammates?"

"That's not what I meant. I see you like to play with people's minds. How about I ask you some questions? See how you like it."

"These sessions are about you, not me. It's best we stay focused."

"Oh no, Doc, you don't get to worm your way out of this. You want to get inside my head, well I want to get inside you too—I mean…in your head," I reply with a sly smile.

"Agent Hunter, these sophomoric antics won't work with me. And what's more, they will not help you in the long run."

I smile to myself and shake my head. She asks what I find so amusing.

"You sit there and act like you know what it's like to be an agent, but you have no idea. We are the ones who have to go out and risk our asses while you sit there in your fancy chair and judge."

"I'm not judging. I get that you, and your team, risk your lives."

I laugh. "Doc, what do you know about risk? You strike me as a woman who has never taken a risk in her life. In fact, I bet you're a strictly missionary kind of woman," I accuse. I wait to see if that gets her. There's just something about her tough, professional demeanor that I want to crack, if only for a few seconds.

However, my rude comment doesn't get to her. Instead, she writes something else down. I get up, shake my head, and take a step towards her. She stands up, uncertain as to what I'm about to do. She looks up at me as I loom above her.

"I bet I'm right, huh, Doc? I bet you don't even wrinkle the sheets, do you?"

"When you are ready to have a real session, please contact my office. Until then, good-bye, Agent Hunter."

"Yeah, whatever, Doc. See you around."

Mia

As soon as Jackson is gone from my office, I grab my water bottle and down the whole thing. My face is flushed, and my heart is pounding inside my chest. Everything about Jackson Hunter says danger. It's not the kind of danger that a woman would run from; it's worse—the kind of danger that women flock to in hopes of getting a taste. Jackson is over six feet tall, with wild, dark eyes that seem to look inside my very soul. He's an endless stretch of muscle and manliness. And yet for all his alpha demeanor and swagger, I sense sadness behind his eyes.

I wish he'd given our session a real shot. I wish he'd put away all his preconceived notions about therapy and given this a real chance. Maybe he'll come around and let me help him. Or maybe he doesn't need my help because he has some amazing woman in his life he can talk to and she has taken care of all his needs.

Why does that thought sting a little?

I start laughing at myself. Apparently, all it takes to get me to forget my professionalism is a hard body and a piercing set of eyes.

Well, Mia, now that you are done ogling your reluctant client, maybe you can get back to work.

I call my assistant, Argo, and ask if my next client has arrived. Argo does exactly what I thought he was going to do—enters my office with a big smirk on his face.

"Oh, honey, please tell me he's coming back. I need more of that man in my life," Argo says. Argo doesn't just work for me; he's also my best friend. I was the first girl he came out to back when we were in high school.

Argo is black and pencil thin, with warm brown eyes and cheekbones most women would kill to have. He's been working his ass off, and now he is only a few weeks away from his nursing school graduation. I couldn't be more proud of him.

He's the reason I haven't gotten six cats and a rocking chair yet. He thinks he can talk me out of becoming a full-fledged spinster. "Argo, is my next client out there?" I ask.

He closes the door behind him and practically dances over to me. "Mimi, girl, you know I know how to be a professional. Okay? No one is out there. Your next appointment doesn't come for another twenty minutes. We got time. So, now I need you to spill all the tea. Start talking."

"Argo, you know that I can't tell you anything about my sessions," I remind him.

"Yeah, yeah, yeah. You took an oath, blah, blah, blah. But those rules don't count because this is a special case. Do you know who just left your office?"

"Yeah, Jackson Hunter."

"Yes, as in one of the five Hunter brothers. Normally, white men don't do it for me, but honey, every single member of that family could get it," he says as he puckers his lips. Argo knows everything that goes on in the FBI building across the street. Well, everything that isn't top secret. He hangs out with the other administrative staff and lunchtime is a gossip fest.

"I've heard a few things about his family, but I wasn't really paying attention," I admit as I take out the file for my next client.

"Well, pay attention, honey. I'll run it down for you. The Hunter brothers are like my grandmother's hot chocolate: rich, hot, and tasty. Each one of them owns a townhouse left to them by their grandfather. And they have a hard-on for charity and shit. But that's just the bio. What you need to know is that only one of them is still single, and you just let him walk out of here."

"What did you want me to do, tackle him?" I laugh.

"To start with! Shit. Desperate times," he mumbles.

"I am not desperate," I counter. Argo tilts his head to the side and arches his eyebrows in disbelief.

"Mimi, let me see your phone," he says as he searches the office for my cell.

"No, there's nothing on there—"

He spots my cell near the window and dives for it. I try to get there before him, but I fail. He gets to my phone and looks at my apps. "Girl, every app on here says 'desperate.'"

"No, they don't."

"You are raising virtual cats!" he says, holding up the screen so that the animated kittens begin to purr.

"Aaron is allergic to cat hair. And 'Pet Pev' is fun for all ages."

"Girl," he says, filled with judgment.

"And I will have you know I don't just have a few virtual cats; I now own the pet shop in 'Pet-Pev' village."

"Oh my God. You need help!" he says as he goes to delete my app.

"Don't you dare!" I plead.

"It's for your own good!" he says. I leap and knock the phone out of his hands; it goes flying. We both make a run for it, but I get there first.

"Ha! I'm faster," I declare like a kid.

"This time, but I'm gonna delete that damn app and make sure you have a life."

"Aaron is my life. And so are you, when you're not being a pain in my ass," I tease.

"You're lucky I have to get ready for your next appointment. This is far from over, missy!" he says mischievously as he heads out into the waiting room. I'm smiling so hard, my face hurts. Argo is such a sweet soul; it's hard not to feel good around him. When Tom and I spilt up, Argo was there every step of the way. And when his grandmother passed away last year, we cried together and held onto each other. He's family.

The rest of the day is pretty uneventful, although I have to admit there were a few times when my mind drifted to thoughts of Jackson Hunter. I was thinking of ways to reach him as a client, but in all honesty, I had other thoughts—thoughts that had nothing to do with work.

By the time my last session is over, I'm exhausted and more than ready to head home. It's Friday, and that means pizza night. It's Aaron's favorite night of the week, not just because he loves pizza, but because I allow him to stay up all night like a big kid. The truth is, he never lasts more than half an hour past his original bedtime. But he likes thinking he's a rebel and that he's staying up as late as the grown-ups.

I gather my things and call out to Argo in the waiting room, "You sure you won't join us tonight? Aaron wants to try something yellow on his pizza. Or at least that's what he said last week. I'm hoping he forgot because pineapple on pizza is just wrong." Argo doesn't reply. I walk out to the waiting room thinking he might have stepped away from his desk. But no, he's standing right there. I hear the elevator door close behind him.

"Was that a delivery guy?" I ask. Argo nods, all the while looking at something on his desk. I can't tell what it is from where I'm standing.

"Did they finally send my new business cards?"

"No," he replies in a whisper. When Argo turns towards me, worry and dread are etched in his face.

"Argo, what is it?"

He steps aside so I can see what the delivery guy just dropped off: a single black rose.

Shit.

He's found me.

Chapter 3

Mia

The first thing I want to do is pack my stuff, grab my kid, and run to the other side of the world. Argo can see the alarm in my eyes, and he knows exactly what I am thinking.

"Just tell me what you want me to pack and where we are headed next, honey, cuz you know I got you," he vows.

In my mind's eye, I am already packed and ready to go, but that's just it, go where? And how long can I keep running? It's difficult to do, but I make myself pause for a few moments and think. Yes, running is the very first thought, but is it the right one? Aaron loves his school; it's been a year, and he's made friends. I am finally building a solid list of clients, and living here in New York City with Argo has been amazing. When I lived in Connecticut, he begged me to come to the city and said that I would love it. He was right. Why should I have to give that up?

"Okay, let's try and stay calm here, okay?" I reply as I make myself take deep breaths.

"To hell with being calm. If Gorman has found you again, then we need to go. There is no way I'm letting anything happen to you or my godchild," he says as he begins to pack up his desk.

"Wait, okay? Let's just wait for one moment. Maybe it's just a joke. Maybe Tom is playing a trick on me."

"Since when was Tom organized enough to even order flowers? This is a guy who used to microwave eggs. He doesn't plan anything. This isn't him. Besides, you and I both know Tom would never scare you. He's not a creep; he's a man-child."

Argo is right. Tom doesn't have one malicious bone in his carefree body. In fact, we would still be together right now had I agreed to act like a teenager forever. Tom is irresponsible and foolish. But he's not cruel or mean-spirited.

"That's true; Tom would never do this. In fact, when Gorman first popped up and began to stalk me, Tom offered to help by looking after Aaron while I dealt with everything."

"It's a good thing you didn't accept his offer. Knowing Tom, he would have traded Aaron for a handful of magic beans," Argo says, clearly trying to cheer me up.

"Okay, let's just think for a second. When Gorman started sending the black roses, it was usually followed by a phone call with him breathing on the other end. And we haven't gotten a call, have we?" I ask, filled with hope. The moment the words come out of my mouth, the phone on Argo's desk rings. We both look at each other. Fuck.

Argo picks up and says, "Don't let this perfect face fool you, bitch, I will cut you!" Seconds later, Argo's eyes go wide, and he places his hand over his mouth.

"Who is it? Is it him? Is it Gorman?" I ask, too terrified to keep my voice steady. Argo removes his hand from his mouth and speaks into the phone.

"Hello, Reverend Worth…yes, we are still planning on helping out with the canned food drive next month. Yes, that's right… Sure, no problem… Good night." Argo hangs up the phone and shakes his head. "Well, I'm going to hell."

"I saw your profile pics on Tinder; you were always headed for hell," I remind him.

"Well, yeah, but shit, I didn't want to go express!" We start laughing. It's an unexpected release that both Argo and I needed.

"So, what now?" he asks.

"Well, we wait to see if Gorman calls. If he doesn't then maybe this was some kind of mistake. Maybe it was delivered to the wrong place."

"Yeah, okay. Maybe," he says. My face falls.

"What?" he says, noting my reaction.

"Can you at least sound like you believe it?"

"I'm sorry. I'm black. That means I was raised to be suspicious and distrust every damn thing. That's what keeps my people from saying dumb shit like 'What was that in the woods; let's go check it out!'"

I smile and will myself to push the dread and fear away. I picture it getting smaller and smaller until it's no more than a dot in my mind's eye.

"Girl, are you visualizing?" Argo asks.

"Yes. I'm taking control of the situation instead of letting it take control of me."

"Okay, well, while you do that, I'm gonna get my pepper spray in case we need to throw down."

I shake my head and speak in a calm voice, "There was no follow-up call. This could be nothing." Argo looks over at me; he reads the quiet plea in my eyes. He knows that I need this to be nothing. He knows the *hell* Gorman brought to my life. Argo pulls me in for a tight hug.

"Don't you worry; I got you. And there's no way I'm gonna let anything happen to you."

When we pull apart, I manage to blink back the tears. I even manage a smile. "There was no follow-up call. Gorman is part of my past. Right?"

"Right."

Aaron and I usually follow pizza night with a movie on the sofa. I want to cancel and just spend the night holding him as tightly as I

can, making sure he's safe. But Aaron would ask way too many questions. He'd wonder why he couldn't see a movie like he normally does on Fridays. And besides, there really is no need to panic because I didn't get a creepy call after the flower came. So, everything is okay. Why should I change our schedule?

"Are we ready to go?" I ask my son.

He looks down at the coffee table to make sure we are all set. In addition to the pizza, he has helped me put out popcorn, juice, and fruit. I know he won't touch the fruit unless I make him. But still, I put it out. We get cozy under a thick dinosaur-themed comforter and get ready to watch the newest installment of *Toy Story*.

I look over at him as he watches TV. The character on the screen, Woody, does something silly, and Aaron laughs with his whole body. There's a spark in his eyes; there's something magical about my kid. God knows sometimes he can really test my patience, but I couldn't see my life without him. I know I can't shield him from everything, and that one day, he'll go out into the world and face hard times. But I just pray to God that he can still keep that spark in his eyes.

"Mom! Stop it!" he says.

"Stop what?" I ask, although I can pretty much guess what he's going to say next.

"Stop looking at me."

"Sorry, but you're very handsome," I reply.

"I know, Mom, but watch the movie," he says in a matter-of-fact tone.

"Okay, okay. One question first," I reply as I put the *Toy Story* gang on pause.

My son sighs dramatically and turns to face me. "Yes," he says.

"What do you know for sure?" I ask.

"I. Am. Loved," he says, tilting his head side to side with each word. That's his way of telling me he knows and that I don't need to remind him. I don't care. I'll remind him every day.

"That's right," I reply as I lean over and kiss his forehead. That's when I notice that the slightly faded "wash off" tattoo on top of his hand has been altered.

"Did you add something to your stegosaurus tattoo?" I ask as I look closer.

"Yeah, Argo helped me put sparkles on it."

"Why does a dinosaur need to sparkle?"

"Argo says *everything* needs to sparkle."

Yeah, that sounds like Argo.

Jackson

"No!" I bolt upright in my bed as if someone zapped me with a live wire. My heartbeat is off the charts, and I'm bathed in cold sweat. I look around; for a moment, I am not sure where I am, and then it comes back to me—home. I'm home. It's just a nightmare, the same one that I have been having for weeks. I rake my hands through my damp hair and hang my head.

Why the hell won't these dreams go away?

The nightmare always starts the same way. My team gets ready to enter the warehouse, and they look for my signal. But somehow there are two versions of me in the nightmare. One version tells them it's clear to enter, and the other version says to stay back. The cruel part is that no matter which version my team follows, half of them end up engulfed in a sea of flames.

I get out of bed and into the shower. The hot water pours down on me and helps relax my tense muscles. But it doesn't take the image of my teammates' burned flesh away. I can still hear them screaming. I know it's in my head, but I swear to God, they might as well be standing right next to me. I go over that day again and again. I look for ways I could have altered the ending, and each time I come up with nothing.

I used to love living alone. But recently, the silence has been getting to me. It allows me to hear my thoughts, and right now, that's not something I want to do. I find myself visiting my brother Wyatt and his wife, Winter, a lot more often. They have three boys and a little girl. They never have a moment's peace or silence of any kind before 8 PM. There is always lots of horseplay and laughter at their place.

So, just do like your brothers have done; find a woman who is gorgeous, kind, smart, and warm. Have kids with her and then settle in for the perfect family fairy tale. Yeah, right.

I'm the only one in my family who hasn't tied the knot. I'm mostly okay with that. The fact is, my job doesn't make it easy to have a personal life. My brothers got lucky—very lucky. They found women who were willing to deal with the life that comes with being in law enforcement. There aren't a lot of women out there like that.

Don't get me wrong; I can't complain about my social life. I can get laid easily enough. And I don't need to string a woman along and tell her that we are together when we aren't. I tell them right off the bat I'm not looking for anything serious. A few nights of fun and then we both move on. So far, there has been no issue at all. In fact, I manage to stay friends with the women from my past. The guys at the office always ask how I'm able to do that.

It's because my dad instilled in us that we were to treat women the same way we would want someone to treat our baby sister, Rose. That just hit home with us, and while we aren't perfect, my brothers and I try not to be total dicks. We succeed—most of the time. And other times, well, let's just say we try.

I didn't really decide to go over to Wyatt's house; I just found myself there. His wife, Winter, comes to the door with her blonde hair pulled back into a carefree ponytail and her robe on. She quickly opens the door and ushers me inside.

"Jackson, is everything okay?" she asks as her sparkling gray eyes fill with worry.

"Yes, 'Mom,' everything is fine. I was just out taking a walk," I tease.

"Hi, Uncle Jack!" my nephew Ben shouts from the second-floor banister.

"Benjamin Lewis Hunter, if you ever want to see your PlayStation again, you better be under the covers in three…two…"

"Okay! Okay!" he says as he runs back into his room.

"Wyatt is on a stakeout. It might be all night. Anything I can do?" she offers.

"No, I just wanted to stop by and say hi."

"Nightmares?"

"Yeah, how did you know?"

She smiles warmly and says, "Easy. I married a cop."

She guides me towards the kitchen and begins to assemble a plate of food from the meal that Wyatt cooked earlier. My brother is an amazing cook. Before my sister, Rose, passed away, they used to cook together. He still keeps that tradition alive although she's gone. He didn't always. At one point, he refused to make as much as a boiled egg. But after meeting Winter, he found a new source of inspiration.

"You sound like you had a hard day; talk to me. How bad was it?" she asks.

"It kind of sucked…" I admit.

Although, there was this one woman who had these eyes, these spectacular eyes.

Chapter 4

Jackson

My shift ended over an hour ago, but instead of going home, I opted for the bar across the street from the office. It's just after six in the evening, and I'm not all that eager to drink. But I'm also not that eager to go home. I sit at the bar and nurse what will most likely be my only beer. I honestly don't know how it is I started to play with the video game on my phone. In fact, I didn't even know I had a game on my cell. But somehow or another, it's on here, and it starts to take all of my attention.

It's a good thing I'm not here to meet women because playing on your cell is not a turn-on for any woman I know. But as I said before, I'm just here to avoid going home, not to pick anyone up. There's a redhead that's been running through my mind, and for now, I'm good with her taking up some of my mental space.

"Damn it!" I shout before I can stop myself.

The game I'm playing is called *Dragon Master*. It isn't all that hard, yet I can't seem to get the little hero past the big giant dragon and through the door to the room that holds the damn ruby. I know it's a silly kid's game, but when I fail to do it a third time, I start to take that shit personally.

"You have to get a head start, run towards it, and jump on its tail three times. That's the only way to kill it!" someone says as they sit down at the bar next to me.

The redhead.

Shit.

"Doc, what are you doing here?" I ask like a teenager caught doing something very wrong and very embarrassing.

"I come here once in a while; they have really good wings," she replies.

"I was just—"

"Playing *Dragon Master*. I know," she says, clearly enjoying my embarrassment.

"One of my nephews must have gotten hold of my cell when I wasn't looking and uploaded it on there. I went to delete it, but I started playing and now…I have to beat this damn thing; it's a matter of pride," I admit.

She laughs and says, "I totally get it."

Her laugh is unlike any melody I've ever heard before. What the hell is going on here?

I try again, confident that I will fail because now I'm way too busy with the woman seated next to me to worry about a stupid dragon. Her fragrance is soft and subtle. It reminds me of a crisp fall morning. And in case you didn't pick up on it, I am losing my fucking mind.

Crisp fall morning?

"Argh!" I shout yet again as the dragon does an animated dance over my corpse.

"Here, let me," she says as she takes my cell from me.

"Are you sure you can handle this?" I ask.

"Don't worry, Agent Hunter; I will rescue you," she says with a smile.

My heart skips.

It takes her only a few moves to best the dragon and get the ruby behind the door. She hands my cell back to me and winks. Or I should say, gloats.

"Okay, okay. You're a real badass. Happy, Doc?" I tease. "Now, how do you know so much about this game?"

"My son, Aaron, loves it."

"You have a son?"

"Yes; he's seven, and I can't count the number of times I've had to threaten world war three in order to get him to put the game down. One day, I was bored at home, and I tried it; don't let the color theme and cute animation fool you. Those fiery dragon bastards are ruthless. It's kill or be killed," she jokes.

"Yes! They pull you in with the friendly graphics and before you know it…"

"Before you know it, it's seven in the morning, and you have not done anything you were supposed to do. And you are forced to send your kid to school with half a frozen Pop-Tart in his mouth and in his Batman pj's."

"Did you really do that?"

"Yeah, that's me—mom of the year." She laughs. I can't help but join her.

"Okay, you have to show me a picture of the kid who's brave enough to be your son."

She happily shows me a picture of Aaron on her cell. He is the spitting image of her. He's fucking adorable. He seriously could not be any cuter if he tried.

I tell her that and she thanks me. She admits he's a handful and says that some days she has no idea if she's doing a good job or not.

"You, Doc? You seem like the kind of woman who has everything under control," I reply.

"Nope, I can only slay dragons; after that, I'm useless," she says. I smile at her wit and easygoing nature. I didn't expect that. I call the bartender over, and she orders wings and beers for both of us.

"Listen, Doc, the last time we met, I was a dick to you, and I shouldn't have been. I'm sorry."

"It's okay. Therapy isn't always easy," she says. "But it can help. I've seen it work."

"I thought about going once a while back when my sister, Rose, passed away. Leukemia."

"I'm sorry. I didn't know."

"It's okay. And thanks."

"So…did you end up going?" she asks gently.

"No…but I did take time off work."

"Did it help?"

"Yeah, I think it did. During my time off, I went camping. Growing up, our parents had a cabin upstate, and we'd go there in the summer. Rose and I would stargaze all night. So I went camping nearby. It helped me feel close to her." I have never admitted that to anyone outside my family before. She is very easy to talk to. Guess that makes her great at her job.

"I get it. My dad was a baseball fan to his core. I can't remember a time when there wasn't a baseball game on in the house. So after he passed away, I found myself watching baseball games. Even if I had no idea what was going on. Sometimes, I would just keep it on in the background."

The bartender comes over and tells us that they are out of the regular wings but that they have the extra, extra hot ones.

"Would you two like to try it?" he says.

"You wanna give it a shot?" she dares.

"I will if you will," I counter.

Moments later, he brings over a basket of "fire" wings and two ice-cold beers. We each pick up a drumstick and take a bite. The bartender was not kidding; that shit is crazy spicy. The heat sneaks up, and soon it's like flames going down my throat. She must be feeling the same way because, like me, she rushes to down her beer.

"Oh my God, what sick, demented person invented wings this hot?" she pleads.

"These wings could be used as a torture device."

"Well, if I had any secrets I'd sure as hell give them up," she says, still panting as she drains her mug of beer.

"Same here. I'm not looking to be a hero," I admit.

When we finally get the feeling back in our mouths and lips, we can't help but laugh at how stupid we must look.

"How do you feel about something sweet right now?" I ask.

"Yes, please," she says.

"Hey, can we see your dessert menu?" I ask. The bartender hands us a small menu, and she studies it over my shoulder. My body is extremely aware of just how close she is to me. I inhale her scent. Fall is now my favorite season.

"How do you feel about molten lava cake?" she asks.

"Never had it," I admit.

"Well, once again, I'm here to help," she says as she places our order. Moments later, the bartender hands us one dessert with two spoons.

"So, this lava cake is pretty special, huh?" I ask.

"Um, yeah. There's chocolate oozing from the center. This cake isn't just special; it's sacred," she says as she's about to sink her fork into the center. I stop her.

"Well, if this cake is holy, then I should at least know the first name of the woman I'm sharing it with, don't you think?"

She smirks as we lock eyes. She blushes and tilts her head slightly to the side. She's thinking. She's so damn cute when she does that. My heart can't take it. Shit. I think I'm in trouble.

"Okay. My name is Mia."

Mia.

"Hi, Mia," I whisper as I gaze into her eyes. She swallows hard. Her lips part slightly as she tries to catch her breath.

"Hello, Jackson."

Mia

It's been a full week since I had the black rose delivered to my office. I'm relieved that we have had nothing else happen to suggest that Gorman is out there. It feels like we can get back to normal. That means hanging out with Argo and Aaron on this chilly Saturday afternoon. Right now, Argo is in my living room flipping through various books on conduct and professionalism.

"I'm sorry; I don't see anything in here that says you can't have wings with a hot guy," Argo announces.

"It's not about the wings. You should have seen us. It looked more like a date than anything."

"Yeah, so?"

"So? Argo, Jackson is my client," I remind him.

"Doesn't he have to attend a session to be your client?"

"He did. Remember?"

"Yeah, he came for ten minutes and then left. There's a grace period. You are free and clear. Get some, girl. Get some."

I laugh. "Argo, that's not really how this works."

"So drop him as a client."

"No, I want to help him."

"Well, if you drop him, you can help him in other ways…" he says suggestively.

"You have a dirty mind."

"Yes, and you know it!"

"Yeah, I do." I grin.

He closes the books and comes to sit next to me on the sofa. "Okay, Mimi. Talk to me."

"What do you want to know? I already told you everything."

"No, you told me what happened: you bumped into him, you two had wings and a drink. But that is not all the tea, and you know it. How did you *feel* when you two were talking? Did he feel like a client? Or something more?"

Something more, so much more.

I'm relieved when Aaron interrupts us. He stands in the doorway, fresh from his nap, Mr. Henry in hand.

"Hi, Argo," he says.

"Come here, cutie!" Agro replies. Aaron walks over to Argo and embraces him.

"Can we put sparkles on Mr. Henry today?" Aaron asks.

"Heck yes! We'll make him up, and he will be the shiniest thing in the reptile world," Argo vows.

"Okay, I'll get the glitter," Aaron says as he runs up to his room. When my son is out of earshot, Argo asks if he's said anything else about his father.

"No, he hasn't mentioned Tom. Thank goodness," I reply.

"Maybe if you gave Tom a heads-up, he'd actually show up," Argo suggests.

"Maybe. But you never know with that man," I mumble in frustration.

That's another reason why this Jackson thing can't actually be a thing. Even if he weren't my client, I don't trust my judgment when it comes to guys. I was so wrong about Tom, and while he's not evil, he is definitely not what I would have wanted for Aaron or myself. In recent years, I've started to believe that there just aren't any good men. But even if there are, who says that I would be good at choosing one? After all, I failed once already.

Chapter 5

Mia

Meeting with my ex always puts me on edge. But Aaron asked me about show-and-tell yet again yesterday, so I thought I should give it a shot. Tom is supposed to meet me here at 1 PM for lunch, so naturally, he doesn't walk in until 1:45. He enters the restaurant wearing his usual boyish grin and laid-back expression.

"You're late," I point out as he moves in to embrace me. I hug him back. It's not a firm, loving hug. It's more like a quick exchange. I never want to think of Tom as an enemy of mine. No matter what has happened, he is Aaron's dad, and I try to remember that and show him some respect. But sometimes he makes it hard. He looks me over and grins suggestively.

"How's my favorite redhead?" he asks as he takes a seat across the table.

"Fine. You know you're late, right? I've been waiting for almost an hour."

"Sorry, babe. Lost track of time." He shrugs.

"It's called a watch—and don't call me babe."

"You know, every day you get more and more prudish."

"You mean 'grown-up'?" I quip.

"Same thing," he says with a smile. "Hey, how's my kid?" he asks.

"That's why I asked you to meet with me."

He leans in and asks a concerned, "What's wrong?"

That's the thing about Tom that stops me from writing him off completely. He loves Aaron. He's just not good at the other parts of fatherhood.

"He's okay. He's got friends at school, he just had a checkup, and Dr. Soul says he's in perfect health."

"Great. I'm gonna come around sometime next week and see him. I miss him."

"Well, I'm glad you said that. There's a show-and-tell at school next week, and he wants you to be there. Can you come?"

"Oh yeah, I'm there," he says, then puts the water glass to his lips and drinks.

"Tom," I warn as I lean in close, "don't say you are coming if you're not."

"Hey, have I ever let you down—don't answer that."

"I'm serious. This is important to him. I won't tell him you're coming. He can prepare to present something else, and if you actually come through, on that day, I will let him know then."

"I'm hurt. You act as if I don't talk to my son. I talk to Aaron all the time."

"Texting me to ask how he is isn't the same thing as talking to him."

"Yeah, I know. But when we hang out, we have a lot of fun together. You can't deny that."

"No, he loves hanging out with you; you two are the same age," I quip. "What he doesn't love is you making him wait and then not showing up. And I'm telling you if you don't show up for this thing next week, I will hunt you down and rip your damn balls off. You got that?"

He leans forward and smirks, "Aw, admit it, Mia, you miss me and what we had."

"Tom, I miss you like I miss my last yeast infection."

"Ouch."

"Well, I was planning to be nicer to you, but I've been waiting here for almost an hour," I remind him.

"I know, sorry."

"What kept you?"

"Actually, it's kind of amazing. I have a buddy in London who is opening an art gallery. He thinks that my work might do very well there. He wants me to come out and stay for a while. Maybe get some work done." Tom is actually a good artist. But he lacks the discipline to finish most of his pieces.

"I know how important having a gallery opening is to you, so good luck," I reply sincerely.

"Yes, it could change everything. The art scene in London is fresh. It's not stale and dull like it is here in the US."

"And the women in London, I'm sure they are fresh too," I add.

"Aw, don't worry; you will still have a place in my heart," he says.

"Yeah, yeah. I don't need a place in your heart. What I need is your butt in that classroom next Friday for show-and-tell at 2 PM sharp. Can you do that?"

"Anything for Aaron and you."

"Good. When will you go to London and how long will you stay?"

"Next month. I have no idea how long I'll be gone, but hey, like I always say, time is just a concept. I have to go there and listen to the city. I have to immerse myself in the people."

"Fine, do what you need to do. Just remember—"

"I know, I know, show-and-tell next week, Friday. Got it, babe."

"Tom—"

"Yeah, yeah, don't call you babe. So, is there some lucky guy who does get to call you babe?"

"None of your business. I have to go," I reply as I stand up.

"Hey, what happened to us actually eating lunch?"

"If you wanted to eat, you should have come at one o'clock, like we planned. I have to get back to work."

"Okay, but you're still paying for the meal, right? I'm starving, and I didn't bring any cash."

Someone shoot me.

I place a few bills on the table; he stands up and kisses me on the cheek. I roll my eyes at him. He studies me and says, "There is some guy, isn't there?"

"What are you talking about?"

"When I asked, you got this dreamy, faraway look on your face."

"There's no one," I reply.

"Hey, whoever he is, he's a lucky guy."

"Good-bye, Tom."

"Bye, babe."

"Tom!" I scold as I march out the door.

"I know, I know…"

Jackson

There are times when being an FBI agent can be thrilling and filled with action. But there are also moments of overwhelming boredom, like this one. We're parked outside of a warehouse run by a well-known mob boss. We've been listening for weeks to get something we can use to indict him, but so far, we have nothing. He knows better than to say anything incriminating, but we listen anyway in case someone on his crew slips up.

I try and keep my mind on the job, but just sitting here in the van, it's hard not to let my mind wander. It used to be that I would wonder about the raid that happened last month. And while that is never too far from my thoughts, I've recently had other things on my mind. I can't stop thinking about Mia, and it's really starting to get to me.

Before we ate together, she was just a really hot woman I wanted to take to bed. But now, it's more than that. I find myself wanting to know how she's doing, what she's doing, and who she's doing it with.

Sometimes, I imagine her playing video games with Aaron and kicking dragon butt. Other times, I picture her having some passion-filled night with Aaron's dad, whoever he may be.

Why didn't I ask her if they were still together? Maybe it's because I didn't want to know. I mean, what would I have said if she'd said: "Yes, Aaron's dad and I are together and deeply in love?"

What if the father is out of the picture? That doesn't mean she's not seeing someone else. Seriously, in what world would a woman like that be single?

On the one hand, I hate myself for not asking her outright. But on the other hand, I really didn't want to ruin the evening by learning she wasn't single. It was nice just to sit and talk to her. I wanted to stay at the bar forever.

And now I find myself wondering things about her: What makes her laugh until she can't catch her breath? Why did she become a therapist? What worries or concerns her? What does she like to do when she's not working? Does she love a night on the town, or is she more of a "night in" kind of girl? She seems like the kind of woman who is always on the go; does she ever make time for herself? Did she eat this morning or was it another frozen Pop-Tart day? Speaking of which, how's her day going so far? How's Aaron? What does he like to do aside from playing video games? Is he an active kid or more of a quiet one?

ARGH!

"Hey, man, you okay?" my partner, Randy, asks from the passenger seat.

"Yeah, I'm good," I reply as I try to focus on the warehouse across the street.

"You sure? You seem a little distracted."

"Just been a long day," I reply.

"Yeah, I hear you. I met this woman last week, and well, she has a friend in town tomorrow, you wanna join us for a few drinks? If her friend looks anything like the woman I met, you're in for a treat," he says.

"Nah, thanks. I'm gonna lay low this weekend."

"That means you already have something else going."

"No, not really. I mean…I don't know. I'm not sure how to read this woman. I want to ask her out but…"

"Really? You've never had an issue asking any woman out."

"That's just it; she's not just any woman."

Chapter 6

Mia

Most days, I have to go into my son's room to wake him up. He mumbles something about getting up, only to go deeper under the covers. I then have to go back into his room, pull off the covers, and open the blinds to let the sun peek through the windows. Getting Aaron up on a school day usually takes two or even three attempts. However, this morning, he is the one who wakes me.

"Mom! Mom! Mom!" he excitedly shouts as he jumps onto my bed and yanks the covers off. I groan and try to roll over, in an attempt to go back to sleep.

"Mom! It's today! It's today!" he says as he turns my bed into his own personal trampoline. I pop one eye open, and the first thing I see is my son's toothy grin. If he smiles any harder, I think he might actually hurt himself.

"What's so special about today?" I ask, pretending that the event of the day slipped my mind. Aaron's jaw drops. He's shocked and maybe even a little offended that I could forget today.

"Mom, it's open again, it's open again!" he shouts urgently.

"I know, sweetie."

"Let's go! Let's go!" he says, pulling my arm.

Aaron's favorite place to go is the New York Aquarium. He can spend the whole day there and never get bored. If we didn't go at least once a month, he'd complain.

The exhibit begins with a tunnel that makes you feel like you're embraced in a coral reef. It's a twelve-gallery exhibit with more than two hundred marine species, including sea turtles, stingrays, and sharks. There are three different kinds of sharks, but his favorite is the sand tiger shark; it is over ten feet long and weighs more than two hundred pounds. They also designed a portion of the exhibit to look like a shipwreck. There are some portals and glass tunnels that the kids can crawl through and play around in.

The aquarium has been closed for a few weeks now for repairs. My little guy was so disappointed. It's as if he feared that the animals would feel slighted if he didn't stop by to see them. So now, after waiting for what seemed like forever, the aquarium is reopening. And it's not enough that we go on opening day. My kid wants to be among the very first in line.

I had initially told him that we could go after school, but it turns out his school is closed today for faculty development day, meaning the teachers will be in meetings all day. So, I moved my appointments around and thought we would make a day of it. Some part of me wanted to ask Tom to join us; I think Aaron would have liked that. But since he's getting ready to show his work in London, I figure he'll be busy. And besides, Tom already agreed to come to show-and-tell at the end of the week, so Aaron will get to spend some time with him later on.

"C'mon, young lady!" Aaron says, clearly mocking the way I habitually call out to him when he won't get up.

"Alright, alright. Why don't you go wash up, and I'll make breakfast?" I reply, willing myself to sit up.

"I know what we can have for breakfast, Mom!" he says. Before I can ask what he wants to eat, he's already zoomed out of my bedroom and down the hall. He comes back moments later with a blue box in his hand. He holds it up proudly and grins.

"Mac 'n' cheese for breakfast?" I ask.

He signals for me to look closer. "Oh, I see. Shark shaped mac 'n' cheese." He nods and raises his eyebrows like a silly villain in a cartoon.

"Okay, kid, you got it!" I reply.

"Yes!" he says as he begins his silly dance around the room.

"There's one condition," I warn.

"Oh no! What?" he says, deflated.

"I have to stop by my office—I won't work, but there are some files I have to get. And you have to promise to sit in the waiting room—quietly—while I make a few calls. And then we can go. Deal?"

"Deal."

Although I won't be taking appointments today, I'm not surprised to see Argo at his desk. He likes to come in when the office is closed, to go over his filing system and make sure everything is where it's supposed to be. I am, however, surprised to see him on crutches with his right ankle bandaged.

"Argo, what happened to your foot?" Aaron asks before I get the chance.

Argo doesn't look us in the eye. Instead, he focuses on the stack of papers in front of him. Then he mumbles something about basketball. Aaron and I look at each other in disbelief. Argo has never touched a basketball in his life. He looks up at us and sees that we are not buying his excuse.

"What? I told you two; I was playing a very challenging game of basketball. I had to get the ball into the circle thing. It was all very dramatic, and that's how I twisted my ankle," he lies.

"Argo, did you hurt yourself doing karaoke again?" Aaron asks.

"No!" he says too quickly.

"Argo…" I scold.

"Alright, alright, fine! It was yet another karaoke-related injury," he concedes.

"Argo!" Aaron and I reply at the same time.

"Hey, don't judge. I did what I had to do to hold onto my title."

"Why can't you just sing and call it a day?" I ask, not for the first time this month.

"Just sing? Are you crazy? You can't *just sing* a Rihanna song. You gotta move. And that's what I did. I worked my little butt all around the stage. Until I ran out of...stage. I tumbled down some steps, and before I knew it..."

Aaron and I try our best to suppress a smile. But soon we are both laughing at him. Argo says, "I hate you both!" but he's laughing along with us.

"Is this a bad time? Or a really good time?" someone says from the doorway.

Jackson.

My heart is now running a marathon. It's no longer happy staying inside my chest. It is trying to break free and run across the street. I swallow hard, and my stomach dips.

"Hi," I reply, trying to sound lighthearted and casual.

"Oh, I forgot to tell you; Jackson called and said he would stop by," Argo mumbles. I glare at him and make a mental note to kill him later. Argo's reading my mind and knows that I will end his life. But Argo doesn't care; he's too busy enjoying the thick tension in the room.

"Hi! I'm Aaron. Who are you?" my son says as he cranes his neck to look up at Jackson.

"I'm Jackson, nice to meet you." The two of them shake hands.

"I heard about you—you must be the *Dragon Master* champion. I heard you're really good at that game."

"Yeah, but I had to try a lot of times," Aaron replies.

"Well, I try too, but so far, it's not working. Maybe you can give me a few tips sometime?" Jackson says.

"Yup! I know where all the secret doors are and the fruit that has the coins inside. I can show you."

"That would be great!" Jackson replies.

Then Aaron spots something at Jackson's waist. His mouth drops open. He whispers, "Is that a gun?!"

"Yes, it is," Jackson says.

"Are you a police officer?"

"Yes. I'm an FBI agent," he says.

Aaron turns to look at me. His little eyes are about to pop out of his head. He's so excited he can barely stand it. "Can I touch it?"

"No, it's not a toy. Guns are very serious and should never be played with," Jackson counters.

"That's what my mom says. She won't even let me get games with guns in them," he grumbles.

"I think that's smart of her."

"Yeah, I guess," he says as he shrugs. "Did you arrest anyone today?!"

"I did."

"Really? For what?" Aaron begs.

"It was a kid about your height. He had red hair and blue-green eyes."

"You arrested him for that?"

"Yup. That's against the law."

"No, it's not!"

"Yes, it is, Aaron. Jackson might be here to arrest you," Argo replies, trying to stay serious.

"No, my mom wouldn't let you do that," Aaron says as he folds his arms across his chest.

"Your mom's pretty tough, huh?" Jackson asks as he kneels down in front of Aaron.

"Yeah."

"Well, then I guess I can't arrest you."

"Nope," Aaron smugly says.

"Too bad, I was gonna let you sit in the cop car and play with the sirens," he teases.

"Mommy! Can he arrest me, please?" Aaron says, unable to stand still.

I look over at Jackson and playfully scold him, "You are an awful role model."

He laughs and then turns his attention back to Aaron. "I tell you what, I'm gonna check in with your mom, and if she tells me that you are behaving, I think we can arrange a ride in the car—without having to arrest you."

"Really?!"

"Yeah, I think we can do that," Jackson says.

"Cool, thanks!"

"Aaron, I'm headed to the vending machine, do you wanna come?" Argo asks as he takes his crutches and heads for the door.

"Are you gonna be here when I get back?" Aaron asks.

"Yeah, I will," Jackson says as he holds the door open for Argo. Now that they are gone, it's just the two of us in my office—alone. That both thrills and terrifies me.

"That's a really cool kid you got there," he says.

"Yeah, I think I'm gonna hang onto him for a while," I joke. "I'm sorry; I didn't have you down for a session. Did I miss something?" I ask.

"Ah, no. We don't have a session."

"Oh, okay. Did you come to make an appointment?" I ask.

"No."

"Jackson, I signed off on you going back to work because I thought you were a little more open to therapy. I know you hate it but—"

"I'm not saying that I won't go to therapy. I'm saying I don't want you to be my therapist."

His rejection shouldn't sting, but it does. In fact, it's a lot more than a sting. It feels like he stabbed me in the chest. That's crazy. I remind myself that it's not personal and that not every therapist is a fit for every client.

"Hey, don't do that," he says as he studies my face.

"Do what?"

"Don't look so down, gorgeous. I don't want you to be my therapist because I want to ask you out."

"Oh," I reply as the hairs on the back on my neck stand up. I feel goosebumps make their way down my arms.

"So…what do you think?"

"We've already had a session, and that makes me—"

"I've never been here before," he says.

"What? You were here a few days ago," I remind him.

"Me? Nope. Never. I was on my way to work, I work in the FBI office across the street, and I saw you. I thought, 'Wow, she's breathtaking.' I came to ask you out. So, is this your office? What do you do here?" he says as if it's the first time we've met.

"That's not funny, Jackson. I can't date a client."

"How can I be a client if I have never met you before today?"

"You know that's not true."

"Okay, your assistant can clear this up," he says as Aaron and Argo return.

"Hi, welcome to Dr. Samuels' office. I'm Argo. How can I help you?" Argo says to Jackson.

"Your boss seems to think that I have been here before. Is that the case?" Jackson asks Argo.

Argo goes over to his desk and looks over the appointment book. "What's your name, sir?"

"Jackson Hunter."

"No, I don't believe you have ever been here, sir."

"Argo," I warn as I walk over to the desk and look at the calendar myself.

"Oh, so you two have cooked this up so that it looks like we never met. Very funny. But we did meet," I reply.

"I'm sorry, what's your name again…" Jackson asks me.

"It's Dr. Mia Samuels," I reply while shaking my head.

"Well, Mia, I'd love to take you out if you're up for it. I would ask you out right now, but I have other plans. You see, all morning

I've been thinking about sea turtles and sharks. But I'm not sure where I should go to see them. Any ideas?" he says.

"Mom, he can come to the aquarium with us!" Aaron says. "Can he, Mom, please?!"

I glare at Argo. I'm sure he had a nice long chat with Jackson on the phone before he came over here. Damn them both.

"Aaron, honey, stay with Argo while I talk to Jackson for a few moments in my office."

"Okay, Mom."

I signal for Jackson to follow me into my office. Once he's inside, I close the door behind us.

"Jackson…"

"Okay, before you object to us going on a date, you should know one thing," he says.

I sigh heavily. "What is it?"

"No amount of therapy, drugs, or treatment can make me feel as good as I do when I'm standing in the same room with you. You don't have to say yes to going on a date with me, but don't break my heart and say no."

Chapter 7

Jackson

She's torn. I can tell by the way she won't look at me. I never wanted to put her in this position. I didn't want to push her. When I called her office this morning and Argo picked up, I took a chance. And while I'm sure he would never betray her confidence, I figured I'd at least get an update on her status. When he told me she was single, I was relieved.

He went on to tell me things that I already knew—Mia's kind, warm, and witty. But he also told me things I didn't know—she counsels at-risk youth, donates a portion of her check to the children's hospital, and volunteers at the local food bank.

But Argo made it clear that the reason he loves Mia isn't just because of her giving nature. He told me that she accepted him and loved him regardless of his sexual orientation. And that when he came out to her, she never once judged him or made him feel unloved. He wanted me to know that she's a noble person and that if I even entertain hurting her, he'll end my life. I laughed and said I understood. I wasn't upset that Argo had threatened me; I was glad Mia had someone so loyal in her corner.

By the end of the phone conversation, I knew I wanted—no, I needed to get to know Mia. I'm sure there are reasons why it's a bad idea, but I don't care. It's not every day I meet a woman like her, and

I didn't want to let my chance slip away. However, I may be alone in this. She's a professional. She spent years getting her license and building her practice. Even if we only had a ten-minute session, she might not want to risk it. She may turn me down because of the way we met.

Or maybe she'll turn you down because she doesn't feel anything for you, dickhead.

I'm not sure how long I've been standing in her office waiting to hear if she will go out with me or not. It feels like forever, but in truth, I'm guessing it's only been a few seconds.

"Mia, say something."

She swallows. Hard.

Our eyes meet, and there's hesitation behind her beautiful stare. I want her. That much is clear. But I don't want to push her.

Maybe you read this all wrong, asshole. Perhaps she just wants to be your therapist and nothing more. And you standing there asking to hijack her day with her kid is a selfish and lousy move.

"Jackson…" She can't find the rest of her words—she doesn't need to.

"I get it."

"Look, I'm sorry. I just—"

"It's okay. I understand. I shouldn't have pushed the issue. It was a dick move. Sorry."

"You don't have to be sorry," she says, trying to spare my feelings.

"No, it's okay. I'll tell Aaron maybe another time. And really, I'm sorry to put you in this position. Won't happen again," I promise. I exit her office, and she follows soon after.

"Hey, Aaron, I'm sorry, buddy. I think I have to work, but you and your mom enjoy the aquarium, okay?"

"You can't come?" he asks.

"Not this time. But you get to go with your mom, and I think if you're good, maybe she'll take you somewhere nice afterward."

"We always go for ice cream—if it's not cold outside," he replies as he looks over at his mom.

"We will see how it goes, but yes—if you are good, I think we can have ice cream on the way home," she says, never once taking her eyes off me. The connection between us is palpable. Nevertheless, she rejected my offer, and I'm forced to respect that.

Argo, who has been studying us since we entered the waiting room, stands up and gives orders. "Jackson, watch the kid." He then points to Mia. "You, outside, now."

"Actually, Aaron and I should be going," Mia says. Argo places his hands on his hips and scowls at Mia. She sighs and follows him outside. She closes the door behind them, but they aren't far enough to get the privacy that they wanted. I can make out what they are saying, although I'm not sure I understand all of it.

"Let me see your phone," Argo demands from the hallway. I turn to make sure Aaron isn't within earshot. He's on the other side of the room looking through a small stack of kids' books on the shelf near the window.

"What? C'mon, Argo, I don't—"

"Mia Louise Samuels. Your phone. Now," he barks.

I watch as she hands him her cell. He looks it over and throws his arms up in the air.

"Two! You added two new cats to your hoard!"

What cats?

"It's not a hoard; it's called a litter. They just came in the other day," she proclaims.

Argo studies her cell closer. "Oh my god—are you dressing the cats now?!"

"It's just a sweater I found in the virtual gift shop. It gets nippy at night," she counters.

"Okay, girl, I need you to stop and listen to yourself," Argo says.

"I hear myself."

"Um, no you don't! Because if you did, you'd be terrified, like I am," Argo pushes.

"It's not that simple, okay? I can't say yes to a client."

"Now you and I both know that's not the main reason you are saying no to him."

"You don't get it."

"Mimi girl, I do. I do get it. But here's what *you* need to get. If you stop here, Tom won't just be a chapter in the middle of your story; he'll be the end of it. And my girl deserves a better ending. She deserves sparkles and orgasms."

"And you're sure this is what is happening here? You barely know Jackson," she reasons.

"What I know is that virtual cats can't make you smile as you did just now when you said his name."

I feel awkward listening in. I walk away from the door, but their voices still carry.

"Girl, I did my homework. I did extensive research on that man. And even if you two don't work out, he'll still be someone you can call if you have a flat tire. Or give you a ride to the airport. And face it, we all need 'airport' guys in our lives," he says, holding her face in his hands and looking into her eyes. She laughs.

"He's already met Aaron; that's way too soon. We didn't even go on a date. What if—"

"All Aaron knows is that Mom has a friend who likes fish. That's it. The man isn't asking you to marry him. Go see some damn fish. Hell, go eat fish sticks together, if he wants to. Just do something in the real world."

She's silent for a few moments and then says, "Okay. I will."

"Thank you," Argo says. He then fans himself with his hand. "Good lord, you white folks are a lot of work…"

They enter the office again, and she comes towards me. When she realizes that I overheard everything, she's alarmed. She leans in and whispers a warning, "If you say the words 'virtual cat' or 'cat sweaters,' I'm calling this whole thing off."

It takes everything in me not to laugh out loud. All I can do is manage a small nod as I usher her and Aaron out into the hall. But as we head for the elevator, I whisper, "Whatever you say, cat woman."

Mia

When we get to the aquarium, Aaron becomes our personal guide. At first, Jackson thought he was just being cute and excitable, but as it turns out, for every question Jackson asked, Aaron had an accurate reply. Jackson is amazed by how much my kid knows until I explain to him this is Aaron's favorite tour and that he's obsessed with sharks.

"He wants to be a marine biologist," I explain.

"He's that certain, huh?"

"Well, Aaron picks other professions also. Sometimes he wants to fight fires and other times he wants to be a wrestler. But he always comes back to working with marine life. Even if that's not what he ends up doing, it makes him happy, so I try to come as often as I can. Although, if he had his way, we'd live here."

"I can see why—this place is amazing."

"You've never been here before?" I ask.

"My nephews have come here often, but not with me. I usually take them camping or hiking."

"Mom, there he is!" Aaron says, pointing to the massive sand tiger shark. Aaron always does silly poses in front of the glass so that it looks like the shark is eating him whole. So, I expected that. What I didn't plan on was Jackson adding to the mix. Soon the two of them are competing to see who could die the worst fake shark death. The two of them get along, so naturally, that scares me a little. But then I remember what Argo told me, and if Jackson is as decent a guy as I think, even if this date doesn't work out, at least Aaron met an enjoyable friend.

By the time we are done with the tour, we're all starving. Jackson asks Aaron how he feels about ice cream sundaes and frozen hot chocolate. I look over at Jackson and shake my head.

"Do you know what you have done?" I warn him.

"C'mon, we just saw a huge shark; we could have been eaten alive. That kind of danger should be rewarded with giant bowls of ice cream as big as our heads," Jackson replies. He takes us to one of New York City's best spots, Serendipity, a famous dessert restaurant that's basically like living inside the mind of Willy Wonka.

Everything inside this place is full of whimsy and fun, from the colorful large toy displays to their giant melting clocks and endless shelves of decadent treats. This place is magic for anyone who loves dessert.

"I've been meaning to take Aaron here but haven't gotten around to doing it," I admit.

"It's definitely not someplace I'd take my kid to every day, but once in a while, I think it would be okay," he replies as we are ushered to our table. Aaron's eyes are twice their normal size as he looks at giant mugs of frozen hot chocolate being served to the table next to us.

"You're thinking about having kids?" I ask.

"It's not something I think about every day, but yeah, once in a while, I think about it. I'm not sure I'd be good at it," he says.

"You seem to be doing just fine," I point out as I look over at Aaron. He's lost in the colorful menu; he's not paying any attention to us.

"Yeah, but this is just an afternoon. I wouldn't want to be the guy who lets my kid down, you know? My dad was always there for us, and I'd want to give that back. That's not always a given with my job."

"Yeah, I get it. I have my battles with 'mom guilt,' and that's in part due to my job."

"What are you feeling guilty about? You two have a great relationship."

"I'd love to spend more time with him, but sometimes that's just not possible with my schedule. Sometimes he spends most of the day with a babysitter. And by the time I come home, he's already asleep. It's like there's just not enough time in the world."

"Well, in case you have any doubts, you're a terrific mom. And Aaron knows that."

"Yeah right. Wait until I tell him he can't have the supernova ice cream sundae he's been eyeing."

I take a look at the menu, and they have actual entrees too. They have everything from foot-long hot dogs to mouth-watering burgers stacked high with bacon. Typically, I would make Aaron wait for dessert, but the fact is, he's not the only one taken by the rich selection of sweet treats. And right now, both Jackson and I are tapping into our inner kid; to hell with waiting, we want dessert now!

Aaron turns and tells us that's what he wants—the biggest sundae they have. After going back and forth, we all settle on a slightly smaller dessert. It's what they are known for—frozen hot chocolate. It's an icy treat that is as big as my head. They add an entire Hershey's chocolate bar on top. And melt a giant marshmallow in the center. It's basically everything a kid or a grown-up with a sweet tooth could ever ask for. We drink it too fast and take turns getting brain freeze. Jackson and I are worse than most of the kids. We even race to see who can finish first. All in all, I can't remember that last time I had this much fun.

After we eat we take Aaron to the park to work off some of the energy he has bouncing around inside him. He makes friends quickly and soon leaves us sitting on a bench nearby while he plays with his new pals. Jackson and I talk, and I swear I don't know where the time went. Soon it's getting dark. I call Aaron and tell him it's time to go home. He doesn't complain, and I think he's finally worn himself out. We get on the train, and soon we are back in my neighborhood.

Aaron asks Jackson to come up to our apartment and play video games. It may sound strange, but I'm glad when Jackson declines. I'm pleased because of the reasons he gives Aaron. He says, "It's late, and your mom has to work in the morning, buddy. Let's give her some quiet time."

What I liked was Jackson's voice. It was firm yet still respectful. He wasn't scolding Aaron, yet his tone was definite and steady. Jackson was the one thing I could never get Tom to be—a grown-up.

Why does that matter, Mia? Why are you thinking these thoughts as if he's going to be around for more than just this one day? This guy has a flock of women somewhere. Guys like that always do. Right?

After Aaron and Jackson say their goodbyes, I send him up to our apartment to brush his teeth and get ready for bed. I promise him that I'll be up there soon to check on him. Aaron cheerfully waves a final goodbye to Jackson and runs up the steps.

Now, Jackson and I are alone in front of my building, and the butterflies have once again taken flight. Being this close to him, without having to be on "mom patrol," feels thrilling. When my kid is around, he's my first and last thought.

But now that Aaron is upstairs, safe and sound, not to mention full and happy, I can let myself relax. I start to think of myself not just as Aaron's mom but also as a woman. A woman who is standing only a foot apart from the hottest man she's ever encountered.

"Thank you for today, Jackson. I had a great time."

"Me too. You are raising one hell of a tour guide," he jokes.

"That I am," I reply as our eyes lock. The smile fades from our lips. What was once a light and fun moment is quickly changing. The air is now thick with unspoken words. He steps closer to me; now only a few inches of air stand between us.

His fingers reach out and lightly make contact with mine. That's enough to make me heady with longing. My heart is pounding inside my ears; my pulse is racing at a speed that might actually require medical attention. I'm so filled with anticipation, a moan escapes my lips before he touches me.

Dear God, I want him.

But when he leans in, he doesn't go for my lips. Instead, he whispers in my ear.

"Good-night, Mia."

Wait, what? No kiss? No kiss? Really?

He reads the displeasure and confusion in my expression. He smiles slightly. "I can't kiss you the way I want to right now." He signals towards the window above us where my son has his face pressed up against the glass.

"Oh…right," I reply. I clear my throat, but it does nothing to hide the longing in my voice.

He looks into my eyes and says, "Don't worry, baby. We got nothing but time…" He leans in and places a gentle kiss on my cheek. The feel of his lips on my skin causes a visceral sensation; my entire body tingles.

Damn, if that's what happens with a kiss on the cheek, what happens when our lips touch?

Chapter 8

Jackson

It's two in the afternoon, and I'm in front of my house, where two cop cars have gathered. I'm watching the woman in the back of one of the patrol cars. Her name is Megan Green. She's eight months pregnant and seriously pissed off at me. She keeps cursing and shouting at the patrol officers and demanding to be let go. My brother Wyatt, a homicide detective, is trying to get her to calm down. I'm not sure he can do it, but if any guy could, it would be Wyatt. He's nice to a fault and has a way with people. I can't say the same about myself.

After a few moments, Wyatt actually gets the woman to calm down and be still. He offers her water, and since she's not in cuffs, she takes it to her lips and drinks. He even manages to make her give him a small smile. Wyatt has one of the officers take Megan home, and then he comes over and sits on the step beside me.

"I thought you said you had the Megan issue handled," Wyatt says.

"I thought I did. Turns out when you kill a woman's fiancé, the father of her child, she doesn't just forgive and forget," I counter.

"You didn't kill Agent Green. You know that."

"I might as well have. And you know what, it doesn't matter what the logistics were, he was my partner, and he didn't come home. That's on me," I reply bitterly.

"You gotta stop doing that. You can't take everything on, man. You do that, and you won't last long."

"Yeah, I know."

"If your neighbor hadn't called the police, what would have happened? Megan busted all the windows out of your car and then tried to get into the house."

"I know what she did. She's upset. I don't care about my stupid car. I'm more worried about her going into labor prematurely. That's why I came out to talk to her. But apparently, I'm not as good at it as you are. What did you say to her?"

"I told her this stress could affect her baby and that I understand what it's like to hate you. As your brother, I barely like you. In fact, I kind of hate you myself," he jokes.

"So you basically told her I was an asshole and that she had every right to hate me and try to make my life hell?"

"Yeah, that about covers it. I told her that if she waited until she gave birth, then I'd help her kick your ass."

"Ah, yes. Family. Gotta love it," I reply with a smile.

Wyatt gets serious. He does that—often. "Jackson, she can't keep coming to your home, threatening you. You know that as well as I do."

"What do you suggest I do? Press charges on a pregnant woman who is grieving the man she loved? C'mon!"

"No, but maybe if you actually allowed us to take her away and process her, it would scare her into focusing on other things—like her child."

"I won't have her arrested, and frankly neither would you if you were in my situation. In fact, none of us would do that," I reply. "Wait, Logan. Logan would put her ass in jail." I laugh. Wyatt joins me. He agrees. Logan, our older brother who works SWAT, would most likely do just that.

"Seriously, you have to figure out what you plan to do about Megan because I don't think she's going away," Wyatt replies.

"Yeah, I know."

"Jackson, Green's death is not on you."

"I could have stopped it. If not that day, I could have stopped it weeks earlier by doing what Megan asked me to do."

"Megan's request was insane. She had no right to ask you that. And it's not your fault for turning her down. Green died doing what he loved. Period. You can't take the blame for that."

I turn to him earnestly and voice the fears that have been haunting me. "Wyatt, if I had done what she asked, her fiancé would still be alive today."

"Green was an adult, and he made his decision. It wasn't your call to make. I thought you were talking this over with a therapist. Are you still dodging her?" he asks.

I didn't mean to smile; it's just what happens when I think about Mia.

"Ah hell, what is that smile about?" Wyatt demands.

"Her name is Mia. She's fucking amazing."

He studies my face, and his eyes grow dark with disapproval. "Jackson, you can't screw the woman you are supposed to be getting help from. God knows you have options, don't do this."

"I'm not screwing her. It's not like that!" I reply, insulted.

"Okay, so what the hell is it like?"

"She's gorgeous. Smart. Funny," I reply. Wyatt suppresses a smile but doesn't say anything.

"What is it?" I ask.

"I've never seen you this excited about any woman before," he admits.

"She's not just any woman. She has a kid. His name is Aaron. He's so damn cute. He has a thing for sharks. And she has cats but doesn't actually have cats." I don't mean to ramble, but I can't help it. "She's kind of nuts in a way because, well, she bought a pet shop, and that's going to cost her far too many coins. She should have waited a little while longer before she invested."

"She owns a pet shop? I thought she was a therapist?"

"No, it's not a real pet shop. Anyway, I think I'm gonna buy her the building."

"You're buying this woman a building?"

"A virtual one. It's in a nice area, and she can freely expand as she wishes."

"Okay, Jackson, I may need to give you a sobriety test."

I laugh and reassure him that I'm fine and that I haven't been drinking.

"Okay, so tell me about this woman who loves virtual pets and motherhood."

I start to tell him about Mia. I didn't plan to tell him everything, but once I started talking, I couldn't stop. I didn't realize just how excited I was about her and the prospect of us. I tell Wyatt all about Aaron and how bright he is and that thanks to him, if a sand tiger shark ever attacks me, I will know exactly what to do. He listens closely; Wyatt is good at that stuff. He says it's because his wife trained him well.

"Any woman who can get you to go anywhere educational sounds like a miracle worker," he quips.

"Shut up; I've gone to places like that on my own."

"I don't think Hooters counts as educational," he jokes.

"Whatever, the point is she's really something."

"As I said, Mia sounds great, but that doesn't do anything for the fact that you still need to talk to someone."

"I am. Some guy with like a hundred degrees on his wall."

"And are you opening up about the raid to him?"

I don't have to reply, Wyatt knows very well that I'm not. He sighs and shakes his head, "Talk to someone, Jackson. If this Mia woman is that wonderful, she can help you...unofficially. Whatever happens, you need to get this out because, believe it or not, Megan isn't the only one who's out of control here."

Mia

Jackson Hunter seems to be taking up more headspace than I am willing to admit. I find myself thinking about him between sessions and wondering how his day is going. I'm not the only one who thinks about him; Aaron has been asking questions as well. He wants to know how long it took Jackson to become an FBI agent, if Jackson can teach him how to shoot, if he can come to play video games, and if his nephews live nearby. The only one who thinks about Jackson more than Aaron and me is Jackson's biggest fan, Argo.

"All I'm saying is that every drop of tea I sipped having to do with Jackson tells me he's hung like a damn horse," Argo says from his seat across my desk.

"You better stop that," I reply as I try to keep a straight face and bite into my burger.

"What? Hell, honey, the streets are talking."

"Well, stop listening," I scold.

"Fine, I will not bring it up anymore. All I'm saying is you best do your stretches." I throw a fry at him, and he ducks it just in time.

"So, have you guys been talking at all?" he asks.

"Yeah, just about every night. He's seeing a new therapist, so he's back on active duty. And sometimes it eats up most of his day, but he always manages to check in. That's kind of nice; you know, that he checks in—not that he has to." Argo doesn't say anything but that goofy smile of his is hard to miss.

"Stop making a big deal out of it, Argo."

"Okay, I will stop."

"I'm serious. We only had one date. And it was a kid-friendly date."

"You're right. I'm gonna stop," he says as he takes out his cell and goes online.

"What are you looking for?" I ask.

"I'm trying to pick out the best color palette for your wedding. I know everyone says spring, but honey, you don't know the kind of magic I can work with a fall wedding theme. I mean, Ms. Martha got nothing on me!"

"Argo!"

"What?"

"You said you would stop getting ahead of yourself," I remind him.

"Yeah, that's why I haven't ordered the cake yet—by the way, we're going with a pink champagne cake with raspberry mousse topping and vanilla buttercream. It's a little rich, but hell, we deserve it."

"That is not taking it slow," I point out.

"Yes it is—I postponed the fitting."

"The fitting?!"

"Yeah, for your dress!"

"Okay, we are officially getting off the subject of Jackson Hunter."

"I'll get off it when you get off," he says suggestively.

I laugh. "You are just the worst!" I reply.

"Well, I try. How's Aaron doing?" he asks as he takes a fry from me.

"He has show-and-tell tomorrow, and he's super excited about showing off Mr. Henry."

"You didn't tell him about Tom coming? Smart."

"Yeah, I figured I will tell him tomorrow morning before school. I talked to Tom on Monday, and everything is set. I'm glad this is happening; I think Aaron really misses having a dad. And it's nice when Tom comes through."

"Speaking of dads…I called mine."

I stop just short of taking a bite of my burger. "You called your father?" I ask, shocked. Argo and his dad have been at odds ever since he came out of the closet. His dad thinks being gay is wrong and that, in many ways, he's lost his only son. Argo acts like he's accepted it, but there are times when I can tell that it hurts him.

"What made you call him after all this time? Details!" I push.

"I talked to my Aunt Sylvia; she's the Wendy Williams in our family. She knows all the tea. She said she thinks he's softening up and that I should ask him to come to the graduation."

"Did you?"

"No, not yet. This was just the initial contact," he says. It's hard to miss the hope in his voice. I really want this for him. It would mean so much to Argo if his dad were there.

"What did you two talk about?" I ask.

"He asked about work, my health, and you. It wasn't a deep conversation, but it was a start. Right?" he says nervously.

"Yes! It's a great start. Just make sure that you two keep it up, stay in touch. Then you can ask him when you're ready. The fact that you are both making an effort means you have a real chance at reconnecting."

"I always heard that he was proud of me for going into nursing; I just didn't allow myself to think it could be true. Can you imagine my dad being proud of something I did?"

"Yes, I can," I reply as my cell buzzes. I look down at the screen.

"It's Jackson; he says we need to talk," I inform Argo as my heart starts to pound in my chest.

"What do you think he wants to say?"

"Well, I'll find out. He's downstairs waiting."

"Right now?"

"Yeah."

"Okay—wait!" Argo orders. He quickly fixes my hair, gives me a sip of his mint tea, and makes me reapply my lipstick.

"Okay, you're good to go!"

"Be right back," I reply while heading down to the lobby. When the elevator door opens, I see him standing there, on high alert.

"Jackson, is everything okay? I—"

He rushes inside the elevator, cups my face in his hands, pins me to the wall, and sweeps his tongue across my lips. He moves in a series of graceful, sensual motions. His skilled, agile tongue claims mine, rendering me powerless.

His eager, demanding mouth ignites an erotic spark that spreads throughout my body. His touch reshapes me, bends my toes, arches my back, and summons a moan from the deepest part of me. "Jackson..."

He drops his head down to the space between my neck and shoulder and buries his face there. I run my fingers through his hair, and he closes his eyes, lets out a feral growl, and says, "Christ, baby, what are you doing to me?"

Chapter 9

Jackson

I didn't plan to go over to her office and kiss her. I just couldn't stay away from her any longer. So I make my way to her job. And I have to be honest: needing to see her, talk to her, and hold her scares the shit out of me. But it's easy to see I'm not the only one who is in uncharted territory. We have been talking over the past few days, and from what I can tell, she has made very little time for dating. Most, if not all, of her time is spent working, raising Aaron, and trying to keep up with Argo.

I wanted to know about Aaron's dad, but I wasn't sure if I should bring it up. Thankfully, she mentioned it during one of our late-night conversations. She told me that he wasn't a bad guy, but he wasn't cut out to be a dad. She casually mentioned that Tom tended to bail on Aaron. That irritated the shit out of me. I understand having to work and letting your kid down once in a while, but to do it to the point where it's a foregone conclusion is bullshit.

I wanted to point out that all the things she's told me about him don't add up to her "he's not a bad guy" theory, but I held back. I got the feeling she was protecting Tom's image for Aaron's sake. And I admire her for that. No kid wants to hear someone badmouth their parent, no matter what issues they may have with them.

It's been hard to get time off in the past few days, which is why we've been forced to speak only on the phone. But weirdly, it's been kind of nice. We've been forced to get to know each other with our clothes on—also a first for me.

There's no doubt in my mind that if she were next to me, I'd have to take her. There's no other option for me. I want her in ways I have never wanted any other woman. So if she were within reach, I'd pull her close, take in her addictive scent, and make her mine.

From what I understand, my brothers were pretty restrained with their wives for one reason or another. But shit, I'm not like that. The fact is, if Mia is anywhere near me, I'd touch, tease, and taste every inch of her. My fingers would find the way into all her dark, warm spots and explore her until she's breathless and shivering against me. I'd take my time and stimulate her in ways that would leave her wet and panting. And when I think of the ways I'd like her to touch me, it's all I can do not to drive over to her place and throw her over my shoulder like a fucking caveman.

So earlier today, when I went to her office building to kiss her, it was because I couldn't take being away from her lips for one more second. But as much as I wanted to take her right there in the elevator, I made myself stop. Hardest thing I've ever done.

Mia isn't just any woman, and more importantly, she's a mom. That complicates things for her because she can't just jump in. She has to think of her son and what's best for him. I get that. That's why I don't just pop up in the middle of the night. But God, it's hard—literally. I'm hard every fucking night just from hearing her voice on the phone.

It's not just physical attraction with her. I love hearing about her past, the best days of her life and the hardest. They usually involve Aaron. She says she can't recall life without her son. But I've spoken to Argo, and he assures me that while she has a hard time recalling the wild times, he remembers everything. I asked her if that woman is still in there. She said that if I worked hard, she might bring a little of that woman back. Shit, I'll do whatever it takes to get a peek at her wilder side.

I wish I could say that having Mia in my life keeps the nightmares at bay, but it doesn't. The good thing is that they don't come as often as they did before. But when they do appear, sleep eludes me for the rest of the night. And even when I am awake, I can hear Megan begging me to help Agent Green. She's shouting at me, asking how I could be so cold and heartless.

I sit up in bed and firmly dip my fingers into my shoulder muscles. I try to massage the stress away. I want to call Mia—badly. But it's just after midnight, and I don't want to wake her. Although hearing her voice would do wonders for me, I refrain from calling.

There is one thing I can focus on that might make the rest of the night bearable: the kiss. Damn, her lips felt so good, it could actually be a drug. I lie back down on the bed, hoping the nightmares will take a back seat to the kiss. They do. And as I drift off to sleep again, all I can think about is the woman whose kiss is saving me.

Mia

Have you ever had a day where something wonderful happens only to have something awful happen a few hours later? Well, that's the kind of day I'm having. After lunch with Argo and the first kiss to end all first kisses, I went back to work. Then about an hour later, I get a call from Aaron's school telling me that he's been sent to the principal's office for fighting.

Aaron isn't perfect, but he doesn't get into fights, and he certainly doesn't start them. When I get to school, his teacher tells me that he pushed a kid in his class named Charles. When asked why he pushed him, Aaron just shrugged his shoulders. His teacher told me since she normally doesn't have an issue with him that there would be no need for further action. She did, however, make him apologize to Charles and he was made to skip recess.

On our way home, I struggled to figure out exactly how I was going to handle it. I have no issue putting him on punishment, but we always talk about what he did wrong so he knows why he's being punished. This time, I don't know why he did what he did, so it's not as easy to discuss.

Now we're seated at the dinner table, where he hardly touches his food. I make him take a few bites so I know he has something in his stomach. He does his homework and tries to watch TV.

"No TV, games, or electronics of any kind. You are on punishment for the rest of the month," I reply. He turns the TV off and heads towards his room. I give him time to brush his teeth and then I enter his room hoping I can get the full story when I tuck him in.

"Did you feed Mr. Henry?" I ask.

"Yeah," he says in a small voice as he gets under the covers.

"Good. And you brushed your teeth well—not just the front, right?"

"Yeah."

"Okay," I reply as I sit on the bed beside him. "I'm disappointed in the choices you made today, Aaron."

"Why?"

"Because you know better than to hit people. Don't you?"

"Yeah, but Charles made me mad."

"Sometimes people make me mad too. Sometimes I want to yell, kick, and stomp up and down. Sometimes I want to throw stuff."

"You do?"

"Yeah, sometimes. But do you know why I don't do that?"

"Why?"

"Because mad is not forever. But the way you react when you are mad, that can last a long time. You remember when you wanted to play with your PlayStation, and I said no because it was time for bed?"

"Yeah, but I wanted to play really badly."

"Yes, and you got mad because I didn't let you play. What did you do because you were mad?"

"I kicked the PlayStation hard, and it fell off the table."

"That was two months ago. Now, are you still mad at me for making you go to bed?"

"No."

"But your PlayStation is still broken, isn't it?"

"Yeah. You said you won't get me a new one until my birthday."

"That's right. You were mad, and so you reacted in a bad way. Now you're not mad, but because you didn't react in a good way, you still have to deal with your bad reaction—your game is broken. Do you think pushing Charles was a good or bad way to react to being mad?"

"Bad, I guess."

"Have I ever pushed you?"

"No."

"Have you ever seen Argo push me?"

"No."

"Do you see people just walking around pushing other people when they want?"

"No."

"Why do you think that is?"

"It's bad."

"Yes, it's a bad reaction. Now, one more time, pushing Charles—was that a good reaction or a bad one?"

"A bad one."

"Do you think you could have made a better choice?"

"Yeah."

"Like what?"

"Tell a teacher he was bothering me."

"That would have been much better. Anything else?"

"Walk away."

"That's another good one."

"But Mom, what if he hurts my feelings—a lot?"

"Sometimes people will hurt your feelings, and it's not fair. Not everything in this world is fair. And if someone hurts you, it's okay to be sad and even mad. When that happens, you can always talk to me or Argo or your friends. You do not hit, push, or put your hands on anyone. That is unacceptable. Do you understand?"

"Okay. Am I still grounded?"

"Very much so."

"Aw, man."

"What did Charles say that made you mad?" I try once again to get the full story.

"He said he went camping with his dad, and I said I went with my dad too. He called me a liar. He said I didn't have a dad."

Damn it.

"Honey, you've never been camping with your dad," I remind him gently.

"I know, but Charles is always saying stuff he did with his dad, and I wanted to say stuff too."

I can feel my chest tighten. *God, I just want to make it better for him. Please tell me how I can make it better.*

I know better than to open my mouth and say what I am about to say. But it's hard to watch my baby in need and not be able to help him. I should at least be able to make it okay. I'm his mom; it's my job.

Mia, don't say anything. You know Tom. He could blow you off at any moment. Don't you dare say anything!

"Well, just so you know, tomorrow I have a very good surprise for you."

"You do?!" he says as his eyes dance.

"Yes!"

Mia, don't say it! Don't say it!

"Guess who is coming with you for show-and-tell?"

"Who?!"

"Your dad!"

"Daddy?!"

"Yes! He wanted to surprise you. So, go to bed and get some rest. Tomorrow the two of you can show off Mr. Henry to the class."

"Really?! Yes!" he says with a grin almost bigger than his face.

I lean in and kiss his forehead. "What do you know for sure, peanut?"

"I am loved."

"That's right. No more fighting, got it?"

"Okay, Mom."

I walk out of his room, and he calls my name. "Mom?"

"Yeah?"

"What do you know for sure?"

"You son of a bitch!" I yell at the top of my lungs as I hurl my cell at the wall of my office. Jackson enters just in time to duck the flying phone.

"What the hell?" he says as he recovers from the unprovoked attack.

"Oh no! I'm sorry," I reply as I rush towards him. "Are you okay?"

"Yeah, but I don't think cell phone attacks are covered by my insurance."

"I'm sorry. I didn't mean to throw that at you."

"It's better than bullets. Argo said you were between clients and that I could come in. Is this a bad time?"

"I screwed up," I reply as I sink down in the nearest chair and place my head in my hands.

"Baby, what's wrong?" he says, sitting next to me.

"London. That asshole is in London! I can't believe he would do this! I told him how important this was to Aaron. I've called him a million times since we made plans for him to show up. He never even hinted that he might have to leave town right now."

"Okay, let's start over. What's going on?"

I tell him about the show-and-tell at Aaron's school. And how I went against my better judgment and told Aaron that his dad would show up.

"And now, two hours before he's supposed to be there, he calls me to say he took a flight to London and he doesn't know when he'll be back. Who the hell does that?"

"Damn, I'm sorry," he replies sadly.

"ARGH! It's not even him I'm mad at, it's me. I knew better than to get Aaron's hopes up. It's one thing to have Tom be a deadbeat, but this time, it's me. I'm the one who hurt him. If I didn't say anything, Aaron would have just been happy to bring his reptile. But no! I had to open my big mouth!"

"Why did you tell?" he asks gently. I recount my conversation the night before with my son. Jackson listens closely.

"I knew I shouldn't say anything until Tom was right there in front of me, at the school. But Aaron looked so sad and hopeless. I just wanted to fix it for him, and instead, I made it worse."

"You were trying to help, Mia. That's what any parent would do."

"It doesn't matter what I was trying to do! My kid is gonna get his heart crushed, and it's all my fault. I hurt him. What kind of mother does that?!" I reply as I burst out crying.

Shit! Crying is the very last thing I want to do right now, especially in front of Jackson. But the more I try not to cry, the more I cry.

He holds me against his solid chest and gently strokes my back. His voice is low and reassuring. "Hey, you are doing a fantastic job with Aaron. And it's not your fault his dad flaked on him. You do everything you can to make sure he's happy and healthy. Give yourself a break."

"I wanted to do better for him. I see the way he looks when he sees a guy with his kids at the park or in the arcade. He asked me one day if there was something wrong with him, to make his father not want to hang out with him. I swear, hearing him ask me that killed me. Knowing all of that, I should never have said Tom was coming. I can't believe how much I screwed this up."

"Hey, look at me," he says firmly as he hands me a tissue from the box on the coffee table. I wipe my face and look at him.

"You made a mistake telling Aaron. But it came from a good place. You wanted to give him the thing that all kids need—hope. And no one can fault you for that. Aaron is a smart kid; he knows how much you love him. And this isn't going to define his entire life. I work cases and see families that are so broken there's no way they can ever be whole again.

"Thankfully that's not you and Aaron. You are raising him in an environment where he's loved, cared for, and protected. What's going to stay with him is how amazing and kickass his mom is and how much she loves him."

"I just don't want him to get hurt. And when 2 PM hits, he's gonna look for his dad and—"

"And it's going to hurt him. But he has a mom who has a superpower—she can make him laugh and make it all better. And I believe you will do just that. Baby, you can't stop him from hurting—not about this. But you can and will be there to make it better."

"Come here," I reply.

He comes closer, and I wrap my arms around him. "Thank you."

"Anytime," he replies.

I'd like to stay in his arms for another hour or three. But I have a client coming in. After that client, I will head over to the school and break the news to Aaron. I don't want him to wait for Tom. In fact, I won't let that happen again. Aaron is a great kid, and it's Tom's loss, not ours.

I straighten up and thank Jackson as Argo enters with my cell. It has survived; thank goodness I have a very strong cell phone case. I'm glad my client didn't see me hurl things at the wall. So, if anyone is keeping score, today I failed at motherhood and being a composed therapist.

I walk Jackson out to the elevator, and we embrace one more time. He pulls me in for another toe-curling kiss. He too has the power to make it all better.

"I need a lot more of that," I mumble, still in his embrace.

"You got it," he says, leaning in for yet another kiss. My head begins to spin, and I'm pretty sure if I don't stop now, I never will. I pull away.

"Hey, will you call me later?" I ask.

"Maybe, can't promise. I have something I have to do," he says as he heads inside the elevator. That's odd. But then maybe it's cop stuff and he can't tell me. Oh well.

I have been dreading this moment for the past two hours, but the time is here. I've just arrived at Aaron's school. I walk down the hallway towards his classroom and hear laughter coming from inside. I peek inside, and my jaw drops. Standing in front of the class is Aaron, Mr. Henry, and Jackson!

The three of them are entertaining the class with the story of how Mr. Henry got to be on the FBI's most wanted list. It's a silly, goofy story that makes the kids howl with laughter, including Aaron. I open the door to the classroom quietly and watch from the sidelines.

"And that's how Mr. Henry, the Iguana, made it to the FBI's most wanted list! So, if you see him, please let me know, and I will catch him!" Jackson vows in a menacing tone.

"He's right there, behind you!" the class shouts. The kids go crazy as Jackson pretends to be outsmarted by Mr. Henry. Aaron has a look of pride that I've never seen him have with Tom or anyone else. My heart swells. I look over at Jackson.

So, that's what you had to do, Mr. Hunter?

He winks at me, and I smile and hold back tears of joy. I watch as he places his arm around Aaron's shoulder and calls him his FBI deputy in training. He asks who else wants to be a deputy. The whole class raises their hands. He laughs and starts picking potential "candidates." It's then and there that I realize I'm falling in love with Jackson Hunter.

Chapter 10

Jackson

My brother, Cash, looks over the case files I've laid out on the table. My team is planning a raid tomorrow on the biker gang who call themselves "God's Wrath." The members claim to be a harmless group of men who enjoy riding motorcycles. They swear they are peace-loving men who enjoy weekend fellowship and community building. We all know it's a bunch of horseshit, and they know they aren't fooling anyone.

The fact is biker gangs are a growing problem, and they have proven to be just as formidable as street gangs and even cartels. Hollywood portrays them as fun-loving cool guys who hit the road and live on their own terms. However, biker gangs like God's Wrath have committed crimes ranging from money laundering to murder for hire. This particular gang is known for trafficking guns and drugs, in addition to prostitution, money laundering, and arson.

"I'm not crazy about you guys going in tomorrow," Cash admits.

"There's been chatter about us possibly coming for them. We know they will be on high alert. But they've been escalating. They're going to war with Hell's Soldiers, so we can't wait," I reply.

"This one right here—the second-in-command," he says, pointing to the file of a large guy with a skull tattoo on his face. "He's the one you have to look out for. You'd think it would be the leader, but no, this motherfucker is desperate to make his mark. He's fought to overthrow the leader for years behind his back. He's pushed for the club to expand. He's hungry and doesn't give a shit what has to happen in order to come out on top."

"Yeah, he's on our radar. We suspect he's taken out at least six rival members. He has more than enough access to guns, but he has an affinity for blades, his weapon of choice. The last guy he cut so badly, he never made it to the hospital."

"They've been moving a lot of product this year; I think they really are trying to step up their game."

"Exactly why we need to go in now."

"I should be there," Cash says, concerned.

"You suck at your job; I'd end up having to rescue your ass."

"What? You wish. Did you forget who I am?"

I laugh at him. He's pretending to be boastful, but the fact is, Cash is remarkable with a gun. He's one of the best in the city. He met his wife while saving her from a drugged-out gunman. He used to go undercover out of the country a lot, but since he's settled down, he mostly stays in the US. Typically, we would try and run a joint task force, but the asshole at the top wants the FBI to get all the credit for this bust.

"Hey, these guys are not playing. I need to know that you feel ready for whatever might go down," Cash says with growing concern.

"When have I ever not been ready?" I ask pointedly. He's about to say something but thinks better of it and remains silent.

"What the hell, man, what's on your mind?" I push.

"Wyatt says you're still blaming yourself for what happened in the raid. I know what that shit is like, and you can't go out into the field with that mindset. It's the fastest way to get killed."

"I know what I'm doing. I'm clearheaded," I promise him.

"Are you?" he says, no longer bothering to hide his doubts.

"Hey, I just said I was," I reply, glaring at him.

He shrugs his shoulders. "Okay, just looking out for you. I know you'd be on my ass if you thought I was going into a raid distracted."

"Yeah, I would be," I admit. I soften my tone and try to remember that we are all on the same side. After losing our sister, all five of us vowed to look after each other even more so than before. Cash isn't saying anything to me that I wouldn't have said to him.

"Cash, I'm good. I'm not sleeping as I should be, but even that's gotten better," I assure him as I walk over to the fridge and hand him a bottle of water. He has a stakeout later tonight, so he won't be drinking beers. He takes it and downs it quickly.

"Good, stay focused. And by the way, there's nothing you can tell me about lacking sleep that I don't already know," he says.

I laugh. "How are the twins?" I ask.

"Loud." He sighs. He and his wife, Skylar, had twin girls not too long ago. The little girls are cute as hell, but they are a handful. Despite the long nights and craziness, it's easy to see the new parents are seriously in love with their kids.

"How do you feel about being a dad?" I ask.

"Wait, where the hell is that coming from? Crap. Did you get some woman pregnant? How is that possible? Shelby would have told us by now."

My sister-in-law, Shelby, is married to our oldest brother. He works for the CIA. While we all love Shelby, she has a talent for putting her nose in places where it doesn't belong. I call her "Endless" because there simply is no end to her intruding on other people's lives. She's like a small puppy that hops around and barks at all hours of the night. There is no tuning that damn woman out. The other thing about Shelby that I hate is that she is almost always right.

"No one is pregnant," I reply.

"So why the question?"

"Well, there's a woman…"

"Oh, the one Wyatt mentioned. The doctor you want to…examine you."

"Shut up. It's not like that. She's wonderful, and she has a son. Aaron. He's a really good kid. But his dad's a dick. He deserves better."

"Are you the 'better' version in this scenario?"

"Maybe," I reply as I cross my arms in front of my chest and walk over to the window. I tell Cash about Mia and Aaron. I inform him that after show-and-tell, we started having dinner together every night. And if we couldn't make dinner work, we'd fit in lunch or even coffee. And when Aaron got off punishment, we ended up having guy time, which for Aaron meant Shark Week.

"Mia was worried he couldn't handle the gore and stuff, but in the end, she's the one who had to close her eyes. Aaron and I would take turns scaring her. One night we got her so good, I swear she jumped ten feet in the air. I'd like to take credit for it, but it was a team effort."

"Wow, does Mom know?" he asks as he studies my face.

"Does Mom know what?" I ask.

"Oh shit, *you* don't even know." He laughs and shakes his head in disbelief.

"Cash, what the hell is so funny?"

"My brother's in love… Ha! You are so screwed."

"Okay, I've had enough of you, get out," I reply as I shove him towards the door. He continues to laugh.

"Wait until Shelby hears this," he teases.

"Get out, get out," I joke as I push him through the front door. "And don't forget to kiss my nieces for me," I shout.

"Hey, one more thing," Cash says. "About fatherhood…"

"Yeah?"

"It's the best fucking thing you'll ever do."

Mia

The past two weeks with Jackson have been phenomenal. We get along as if we have known each other all our lives. What's more important, he's become Aaron's partner in crime. Seeing the two of them together always picks up my mood.

A few nights ago, Jackson was waiting for me when I got home. I had sessions back to back and didn't even get a lunch break. My head was pounding, the train was delayed, and I had a mountain of paperwork waiting for me back at the office. I'd defrosted some ground beef and intended to make lasagna, but I was so tired, I knew I'd probably end up ordering out. I scolded myself for not placing the order before I got home. I knew Aaron was most likely starving.

However, there was no need to place an order because when I got home, Jackson and Aaron were already eating pizza. It turns out the babysitter had a big test to study for, so when Jackson stopped by, he told her she could leave early and that he would take care of Aaron. The two of them went over his homework and then had dinner. All I had to do when I got home was eat dinner and relax. He even tucked Aaron in for me—per Aaron's request.

The only part that I wish I could change is our schedule. I wish Jackson and I had more time with each other. I've talked to Argo about it, and he thinks that as soon as Aaron is in bed, Jackson and I should go to bed too. But I've never had a man stay the night before, and that's a little scary for me. Well, not just me; I worry about how Aaron will take it. I know how much he likes Jackson but what will he think if Jackson spends the night?

"Girl, that boy loves Jackson. He'll be fine with it," Argo insists.

"I want to go slow with this."

"It's been weeks, and you two have been making out on the sofa when Aaron isn't in the room like teenagers. You two need alone time. I mean, how far can you push a man? I bet he's fifty shades of blue by now," Argo teased.

Ever since that conversation, Argo has been trying to get me to let Jackson spend the night by sending me songs that have to do with people being horny and giving in to their desire.

I think the romance gods must have heard my prayers because as soon as I put Aaron on the bus this morning, I got a text from Argo letting me know that two of my clients canceled. I have the morning free. I decide to surprise Jackson at his house. But then I think of all the movies I've watched where a woman surprises the guy, and it ends up blowing up in her face. So I call Jackson first, and he laughs and says, "Get your sweet ass over here now!" So I hang up and make my way to his place.

Although I've been at his place before, I always marvel at his high ceilings, exposed brick, and the spectacular view. The townhouse his grandfather left him is stunning. I joke that if I knew he was really that rich, I would have given myself over to him already. He laughs and says he'd give away his fortune if I'd stay the night. He's kidding—mostly.

"You look very professional. I feel like we're headed for a session," he teases.

"Sorry, I have to head to work after this, so…"

"It's okay, baby. I'm just glad I get to see you," he says as he pulls me in and takes my breath away with his all-consuming kiss.

He says he's going to jump into the shower and that he'll be right back. I can't help it; I tidy up as I wait although his place isn't messy to begin with. I go over to the dining table and find about a dozen open files. There are pictures of hardcore looking men with tattoos and scars. They all look like they could come to life and damn near rip my throat out. I read off a few lines concerning their cases.

"Oh no, you can't look at that. These are active cases," he says as he enters the room and sees me poring over the files. He quickly gathers them, puts them in a box, and closes the lid.

"I'm sorry. I wasn't trying to pry."

"It's okay. I had them out because Cash came by and he had info I needed. But I should have put them away. Don't worry about it. It's not your fault."

I take in his eight-pack abs and hard pecs. He watches me and gives a warning, "You better stop looking at me like that; I'll never let you leave for work." He pulls me close. I can smell the fresh soap scent on his skin. His hair is still damp from the shower. And when he lowers his head to kiss me, I want more than anything to pull that towel from around his waist.

But before I give in to my urge, I recall the faces from the file. And some of the phrases I read. A dark cloud rolls in, and I feel a cold pool of ice form in the pit of my stomach.

"What is it, baby?" he asks.

"The people in that file…are they in a gang? I'm guessing they are, right? Biker gang?"

He furrows his brows and inhales deeply in an unmistakable gesture of disapproval

"It's a gang?" I push.

"I can't talk about it. I'm sorry. You get that, don't you?"

"Yeah, I do. I can't talk about my clients. It's against the law."

"Yes, well my job is that same way. At least with active cases," he explains. Then he starts kissing my neck and asks, "Now, where were we?"

"How dangerous is this gang?"

"I can't talk about it," he says again.

"Yeah, yeah. Okay. I get it."

"Good," he says. He starts to nibble my earlobe, and a current of lust runs through me; however, it's not enough to turn my mind off.

"Are you investigating them? Is that why you're looking at their file?"

"Mia!" he says, exasperated.

"I'm sorry. I know you can't talk about it. But…"

"But what?" he pushes.

"I saw some stuff in that file: assault with a deadly weapon, arson, and murder."

"You weren't supposed to see that."

"But I did," I reply as I lean on the edge of the dining table.

"Mia, what's going on?"

"You're a cop," I reply mostly to myself.

"You knew that already," he reminds me.

"Yeah, I know, but now…now it's in my face. You are going to face off with these guys. You could get hurt, Jackson." His expression softens as he reads the fear in my face.

"You're worried about me."

"Yes, of course I am. What happens if they attack you or if…I don't know. There are a number of things that can go wrong. Do you guys go in with enough backup? How do you know how many of them there will be when you go to arrest them? That's what you're planning right, to raid them? Yeah, I know, you can't tell me. But you can at least tell me if you will have ample backup. Are you going to be safe? I mean, how do we know that there won't be more gang members hiding out somewhere waiting to attack and how do we—"

"Baby, just relax," he says as he takes my hands in his.

"I'm sorry. I just…I didn't mean to freak out on you."

"It's okay. It means a lot to me that you care enough to worry about me. But I will be just fine. We never go in without being ready on all fronts. I know it can be hard to take in, but this is what it means to be with me. I hope like hell you're okay with that because I don't want to lose you."

"You have to be safe. I mean it. No superhero bullshit. Aaron and I…" I can't finish my thought, but I think he already knows what I'm trying to say. He smiles warmly.

"You and Aaron are important to me too. I will do whatever I have to do in order to come back safe to both of you. I promise," he says as he leans in and caresses my cheek.

"Okay. Thank you," I reply as I literally try to swallow my fears away.

"You okay?" he asks.

"Yeah, but I still can't get their faces out of my head. Especially their cold empty eyes."

"Well, then it's my job to make sure your mind is focused on something else."

He places his hands around my waist, picks me up, and sits me down on top of the table. He kisses me fervently as he lays me flat on my back. He slides his hand under my skirt and slowly glides my panties down to my ankles, leaving a trail of searing heat along the way. He lightly strokes my inner thigh with his fingers then again with his lips. The tantalizing sensations shooting through me are almost more than I can take. When my breathing gets choppy, he knows I'm ready. He pulls me closer to the edge, grabs a chair, and sits at the table; that way my pussy is literally being served up to him.

His warm, silky tongue dances along the edge of my opening. He slides his mouth up and down my folds until the friction sends jolts of pleasure zooming down my spine. I gasp as he buries his face in my pussy. He skillfully moves his agile tongue in ways that make it impossible for me to keep my hips still. The suction from his mouth is so delicious that my body can't comprehend the degree of ecstasy he's bringing to it. In an attempt to stop from being pulled under the tidal wave of passion, I latch on to the sides of the table.

I try to close my legs so that I can manage the flood of desire coursing through me. But he won't let me. He pins my legs open and dives even deeper inside me. He flicks the tip of my clit and coaxes it to the surface.

"Oh…please! Please!"

My cries only spur him on more. He's on a mission: to explore every inch of my pussy until I am soaking wet and damn near pass out from pleasure. It's going to happen. I can't hold on anymore. His control over my body is unparalleled. He glides the flat surface of his tongue over my pulsating clit and sends me to the edge.

"Ohmygod! Ohmygod!" I groan as the frenzy grips me. Every part of my body is being made to bend to the will of this imminent orgasm. Knowing I'm on the cusp, Jackson suckles on the tip of my clit and then flicks it with his tongue at just the right angle.

"Ohmygodimcomingsohard!"

And I do; I come harder than I have ever come in my life. My body jerks uncontrollably. My vision blurs. I moan Jackson's name as he claims my body and greedily laps up my juices.

I swear if I didn't have a mortgage to pay or a kid to feed, I would have stayed on that table forever. But since I do have those things, I grab a quick shower at Jackson's place and prepare to head to work. Before I make it out the door, he takes me in his arms and says, "Mia, you belong to me, don't you?"

It never even occurs to me to argue. "Yes, I do."

"Good, because I damn sure belong to you," he says as he kisses my temple. I feel good. I'm drained and could sleep for days, but I feel good. And as I head to work, I'm grateful for everything I have in my life: my son, my man, and my friends.

I step into the elevator of my office building. I look at the time on my cell. I have about twenty minutes to get ready for my next client. That means I have just enough time to gossip with Argo. I won't tell him everything, of course, but just enough to girl talk. But when I step into my office, I am frozen in shock as I look around. Every inch of my waiting room is covered with black roses.

I look over at Argo. He's standing in the doorway of my office. "I got here ten minutes ago. The door had been pried open. There are roses in your office too."

Before I can find words, the phone on Argo's desk rings. I pick it up and put the phone to my ear. I speak in a soft, breathless tone.

"Hello?"

All I hear on the other end is heavy breathing.

A cold chill rushes through me.

"Gorman?"

"Hello, Mia. Been a long time…"

Chapter 11

Mia

Gorman's voice cuts through me like a hot knife through butter. I hear someone screaming and cursing; it takes a few seconds for me to realize that someone is me. I tell him to leave me the fuck alone. I scream it like my life depends on it—because it does. Argo grabs the phone from me and threatens Gorman. He vows to cut his balls off and feed them to him if he ever calls my office again. He then pulls the phone cord from the wall. I don't realize I'm shaking until Argo points it out.

"Come over here. Sit down, Mimi."

"Aaron! What if he knows where Aaron goes to school?!" I yell. I quickly dig in my purse, searching for my cell phone. I need to call the school and make sure my son's okay.

"I can't find it! I can't find my damn phone!" I shriek.

"It's okay. I got you, honey. I got you. I'm dialing now," Argo says as he takes out his cell and calls Aaron's school. Argo sometimes picks Aaron up, so he has the school's main office on his cell as well as the nurse's office. He asks to speak to Aaron and says it's an emergency. They must have given him pushback, but Argo is unyielding.

"I need to speak with Aaron Samuels, right now!" he demands. It feels like forever before they put him on the phone. Argo puts it on speaker so we both can hear.

"Mom?" Aaron says, sounding annoyed. I'm so weak with relief my knees can barely hold me up.

"Hi, baby."

"Mom, what is it? Mr. Ross is showing us how to turn a soda bottle into a boat and make it move like a rocket with baking soda! It's a baking soda rocket, Mom!"

"Wow that sounds like fun," I reply, blinking back tears once I realize he's really okay. "Honey, did anything…silly or crazy happen to you today? Or did you see anyone that you recognize from a long time ago?"

"No, Mom, can I go now? Please?"

"Yes, honey. Go ahead."

"Okay, bye Argo!" he says.

"Bye!" Argo replies. He hangs up, and we embrace. When the main office comes back on the line, I tell the office to make sure that Argo and I are the only people they ever allow to take out of school.

"Girl, you are still shaking. Sit down." Agro says once I hang up.

"I can't. I can't be anywhere near these flowers." I quickly walk out of the office and into the hallway. Argo follows me.

"I'm here, tell me what you need," Argo says.

"How the hell did he find me? We're gonna have to move again and I—"

"No! Don't even go there. It's not like before."

"Yes, it is! It's exactly the same thing!"

"No, it's not! You have something you didn't have three years ago: Jackson."

"Jackson…" I mumble, mostly to myself.

"Yes, you have to tell him so he can help you."

"No, I can't do that."

"What? Why the hell not? And please do not tell me you are one of those silly-ass women who are afraid to ask for help. That's weak.

You need to speak the hell up. I know I didn't teach you to be no damn wallflower," he demands.

"No, it's not that."

"Then what is it? Why can't you tell Jackson that Gorman is after you?"

"Do you remember what Gorman did to the last guy he saw me with?"

"Damn…" Argo says as it all comes rushing back to him. "But Jackson can handle himself. You've seen him. You don't think he can take this on?"

"Yes, he can. But he shouldn't have to."

"So, what are you gonna do? Just pretend this didn't happen? I'm not gonna co-sign that move. Sorry. We need to deal with this fucker!"

"Yes, and we will. We'll go to the cops; we'll change the locks, get video cameras for the office and my apartment, the works. Okay?"

"No, not okay. We need Jackson. *You* need Jackson."

"Argo, please, I need to handle this my way. I can't let him get involved. He doesn't deserve that."

"And neither do you."

"I know. And I will tell him, once the cops find Gorman. Maybe this time they can get him and make it stick. Okay?"

Argo sighs and folds his arms across his chest. "I tell you, some men are just fucking evil. Hey, I got an aunt down in Louisiana, you say the word, and I will have roots put on him."

I didn't expect Argo to say that. I burst out laughing despite my terror.

"Don't laugh. One call from me and my aunt Eula will have that man visited by pissed-off ghosts of former slaves. He'll be in the corner tearing his eyeballs out and eating his own hair. You just say the word!"

"Okay, we'll say that's plan B," I reply as I dig in my purse, once again looking for my cell phone. "Found it!" I say. I dial the police. I am determined to be proactive. I will not let Gorman fuck up my life—not this time.

"The cops are on their way," I inform Argo.

"Good, let's wait downstairs. It's creepy here," Argo says. I gladly follow along. Once we're outside his cell rings. "Hi Jenna, I can't talk now … What? … High-speed chase… where? … Okay, thanks." He quickly hangs up and goes online.

I roll my eyes. His friend Jenna loves going online and looking at videos of crazy fights and botched bank robberies. I once saw her actually make popcorn to watch a high-speed chase on the news. Crazy.

"Doesn't she ever get enough of Facebook Live? What is it this time? A fistfight at the checkout counter or elderly shopper pelts 'would be' thief with diabetic candy?" I ask. I know it's a crazy time to be lighthearted, but I'm determined not to give in to the fear growing in the pit of my stomach.

"Oh my god, you have to see this," Argo replies. The sound of sirens blares from the video he's watching.

"No, I'm not into in high-speed chases."

"Yes you are—Jackson's driving."

Jackson

New York City is an awful place to have a car chase. I know that even as I get in the truck and pursue Skull, the second-in-command of the God's Wrath biker gang. He's gotten on his bike and is now tearing down the street. The only reason I'm on his ass is the revelation I had last night.

I was studying Skull's file, and something jumped out at me. He managed to get away from at least three major raids in the past two years. No one would be that lucky unless they had a plan B ahead of time. So, I got my hands on the floor plan of the clubhouse we were going to raid. It didn't reveal anything, but then I sought out the original floor plan for the property. It turns out, the clubhouse used to be a hotspot during the prohibition days. That meant they could very well have tunnels under the floor. Maybe that's how Skull kept getting away.

There was no time to test my theory, so we went ahead and executed the raid as planned. The only difference is I drove a few blocks down and searched for Skull near what I thought would be the end of the line for the tunnel. My hunch was right. I got out of my car just in time to see Skull crawl out from a small opening at the base of the bar. He got onto his awaiting motorcycle. I aimed my weapon and ordered him to get off the bike. He glared at me while considering his actions.

"Skull, don't do it!" I warned.

He sneered and careened down the street in a hail of exhaust and white smoke. I quickly jumped back in my car as a small crowd gathered. I was being recorded. Fucking camera phones.

I call for backup as I follow him. Skull blows through traffic lights and just misses colliding into other motorists and pedestrians. He weaves in and out of lanes, drives in the opposite direction of traffic, and, at one point, goes up onto the sidewalk, nearly mowing down a family.

"Fucking asshole!" I spit as I try to keep up with him and refrain from endangering any more civilians. We have to end this, now. Lucky for me, Skull miscalculates an upcoming turn; the bike goes right, and Skull's body goes left. I pull over, get out of the car, and run towards him. He is injured and limping slightly, but that doesn't stop him from trying to get away.

Seriously, man?

I take off after him. I don't mind a foot chase. It's a lot less dangerous than chasing him in a car. There is less of a chance for collateral damage.

Skull runs down a row of narrow back alleys, desperately looking for somewhere to go. So far every back door he tries to pull open is locked. I'm on his heels, and he knows it's only a matter of time before I catch up to him. He tries one more back door in the alley; it opens into a laundromat.

This cannot become a hostage situation. I will not let that shit happen. I fire into the air, knowing New Yorkers will not need a second prompt. Right away, people scatter out the front door and take cover. I follow Skull inside, and I'm relieved that it's just the two of us. He fires at me, and the bullet zips just above my head. I take cover behind a row of large dryers. He takes another shot, and it lands along a row of colorful plastic chairs. I return fire, and he takes cover.

I spot him in the reflective surface of one of the washers. He looks down at his gun and swears. He's out of bullets. He takes out his trusty blade and crawls behind the small island that serves as the attendant's desk. I aim at the TV mounted on the wall just above him. He protects his head with his hands, but not in time. The TV falls and knocks him down. I walk over to him, weapon out, ready to fire if need be.

He's on the floor, bleeding from his head and moaning about needing medical attention. I tell him he will get it, but first, he needs to place his hands above his head. Then out of nowhere someone scurries out from the corner near Skull—a civilian with a camera. She's in Skull's line of sight. I know what he's going to do even before he does it. He reaches out for the woman's foot, and she falls forward onto the floor. He drags her in front of him, trying to use her as a shield. And yes, she's still recording.

I swear if the lady survives this, I'm gonna kill her ass myself.

"Drop your weapon, or I'll snap her fucking neck," Skull says, seething.

"Okay, let's just stay calm," I reply, slowly kneeling down to place my weapon on the floor. Skull starts to breathe easy. That's a mistake. I pull out the ankle gun I always keep with me and shoot him in the leg. The pain is intense. He lets go of the lady. She runs for her life. I go to handcuff Skull, who pulls out a blade and stabs me in the lower stomach.

FUCK!

The pain does not divert me, but it does piss me off. I apply pressure to the wound with one hand, attempting to stop the bleeding. With my other hand, I place my gun between Skull's eyes.

"Try me," I dare him.

Seconds later, backup appears, and things get very loud and very chaotic. But the most important thing is that we have that asshole dead to rights. As the paramedics appear, one of them comments to the other, "This shit is all over Facebook Live." I have a thought as I get into the ambulance: what if Mia saw this go down? But I then dismiss it. I mean, what are the chances?

My girl has just charged into the hospital room, and it's safe to say she's not happy with me. I want to tell her that my brother, Wyatt, is standing behind her, but she doesn't give me a chance because she launches right into a tirade.

"Jackson Hunter, you promised me that you would try and NOT be a damn hero! You lied to me!" she snaps.

"Baby, I—"

"Oh no, don't you dare call me baby. Lucky for you, your doctor already told me you were okay. Had it not been for him, I would have come in here expecting to see you laid up and dying."

"I'm okay, baby. I just got a few stitches," I reply.

"Oh, so then I guess everything is fine? Are you kidding me? You went after a biker with no backup whatsoever!" she says, folding her hands across her chest stubbornly.

"I know but—"

"I'm not done! Do you have any idea what it was like to watch you play hero all over New York City? There were moments when I could actually see my damn heart fly across the room. How could you just go off and do something so reckless? Is that your idea of fun? Do you think what you did was heroic and exciting? Because let me tell you, it wasn't. And there is nothing heroic or exciting about attending your funeral!"

"Mia, you probably know—"

"And one last thing," she says as she comes closer to the bed. She kisses me feverishly and wraps her arms around me. "Please don't do that again. Or I'll kill you myself."

"I'll help you," Wyatt says, speaking for the first time. Mia practically jumps out of her skin when she hears someone else in the room. She turns to see him and her cheeks grow red.

"Oh, I'm sorry. I didn't know Jackson had—"

"It's okay. I'm his brother, Wyatt. And you had the right idea. He was reckless, and next time you have my permission to beat the crap out of him. Or end his life altogether," Wyatt assures her. She smiles.

"That's my girl, Dr. Mia Samuels," I say. The two of them shake hands.

"When does the rest of your family get here?" she asks. Wyatt and I exchange an amused look. Mia reads our expressions and asks why we're smiling.

"A shallow knife wound doesn't really ring any alarms in our family. In fact, to get a phone call or even a text, there should be internal bleeding and the possibility of losing a limb," Wyatt replies.

"He's right. Being stabbed doesn't get much attention in a family of law enforcement. However, not calling your mother for a month gets a lot of attention," I quip.

"Are you serious? You haven't talked to Mom for a month?" Wyatt asks. I look away. Like the rest of my brothers, we love our mom very much. She's a badass. But time got away from me, and well, now she's gonna make me pay.

"I meant to, but it's been kind of busy," I reply.

"Did you pack yet?"

"Pack for what?" I ask.

"The guilt trip she's gonna send you on."

Both Wyatt and Mia laugh at me. "Nice, make fun of a man who almost died today," I reply.

"Surface wound, drama queen. And don't think that's gonna get you out of having to come to dinner next week and dealing with Mom after not calling her for weeks," Wyatt counters.

"Yeah, well I have a secret weapon, one that is guaranteed to make Mom smile," I reply.

"What's your secret weapon?" Mia asks.

"You. I'm taking you and Aaron to dinner at her place," I reply as I take her hand in mine.

"Me?! Why do you think I can make her smile?"

"Of course she's going to smile; she's meeting the woman her son is in love with."

Chapter 12

Mia

In the past few days, things have been hectic, to say the least. I filled out a police report; they actually have an officer on my case, Officer Peterson. He interviewed me, and I gave him as much info as I could. He seemed far more interested than the other cops I've dealt with in the past. That helped give me some kind of peace of mind. I also had the locks changed in my office and my house.

I had a cleaning crew come in and clean my office from top to bottom. I changed my cell number. I changed the route that I walk from the train station to my office. I also upgraded my alarm system; it now includes video and motion detectors. I have a private car service take Aaron to school and bring him back.

I also deleted what little social media presence I had. I bought some mace, and a friend of Argo's helped me get a Taser. I don't know if that's enough to stop Gorman, but at the very least, he will have to work harder to get to me.

Doing all of the above took a lot of my time. And I still had to meet with clients and look after Aaron. The one who got the short end of the stick in this whole thing was Jackson. I feel awful about it. I know somewhere in the back of his mind, he's wondering if I'm pulling away and not spending as much time with him on purpose. I think back to that night at the hospital when he said he loved me; I could feel my heart growing. I love him too; it's surreal to think just how much I love him.

I haven't said it back to him. That's partly because I've been so busy that I haven't had the time. I mean, saying "I love you" for the first time isn't exactly something you can text. And there's the other reason why I haven't said it out loud. I have to stop and figure out how Aaron factors into this. I don't want him to feel like Jackson is taking his mom away.

It's been Aaron and me for the longest time; will he be okay with it being the three of us? I know the two of them have spent a lot of time together. But I think once you make it official, it's different. I just want to make sure that Aaron is good with it—I mean, really good with it.

I need to find out what he thinks of Jackson and me being officially together. I'm more nervous than I thought I would be as I knock on Aaron's door. When I enter, I find him under the covers waiting for me to come in and say good night. I go over and sit beside him on his bed.

"Did you have a good day today?" I ask.

"Yeah, kind of. I lost Captain America's shield. It fell down the drain. But then I found the purple SpongeBob gum that I stuck under my bed to eat later."

"Did you eat it?"

"Yeah, it was hard but still tastes sweet. And I think I know what I want to be for Halloween."

"You do? Last time we talked about this, you wanted to be seven different types of sharks. Have you narrowed it down?"

"Yup, I'm gonna be a hammerhead or the bull shark."

"I know the hammerhead. What's so special about the bull shark?"

"It eats everything! And it can go into fresh water or salt water."

I study him and the gleam in his eyes. I love this kid so much, and sometimes I think my heart will just burst open when I see him.

"Hello! Earth to Mom!" he says, waving his hands in my face.

"Sorry. I was just thinking that I have such a smart kid. How'd I get to be so lucky?"

"Mom!" he complains as I lean in and ruffle his hair and kiss his cheeks.

"Sorry, I can't help it," I reply.

"Did you see my new book?" he says as he takes a big book of illustrations out from his nightstand.

"No, I didn't see it. Who gave you that book? Did you borrow it from the school?" I ask.

"No, Jackson got it for me."

"Really? I didn't know that."

"Mom, some things are just between us guys," he says in a sobering tone. I suppress a laugh and nod in agreement. That is the best opening I'm ever gonna get, so…

"What do you think of Jackson? You like him?"

"Yeah, he's great! Do you think he likes me?" he asks.

"No, I don't think he likes you. I think he loves you! He's always asking about you when he hasn't seen you. And he loves spending time with you," I promise him. Aaron wears a proud smile.

"I love it too," he replies. Then he looks down at the floor and bites his lower lip. This can't be good. My heart skips. Crap, what if he likes Jackson, but doesn't want him in our lives?

"What is it, honey?" I ask, keeping the worry from my voice.

"If I keep hanging out with Jackson and make him my friend, will Daddy be mad at me?"

Phew!

"No, not at all. You know what your dad wants more than anything in this world?" I ask.

"What?"

"That thing you have on your face right now," I point out.

"What thing?" he asks.

I hand him the nearest reflective surface—the back of a handheld video game.

"You see that smile on your face, that's what your dad wants. He wants to see that you are happy. Does Jackson make you happy?" I ask. He nods his head enthusiastically.

"What about you, does Jackson make you happy?" he asks.

"Yes, he does." I bite my lip and lower my eyes. Now I know where Aaron gets it. "What I wanted to tell you was that I think Jackson and I are in love."

"Okay," he says simply.

"Okay?! Do you know what I mean by that?"

"Yeah, he's your boyfriend, and you're his girlfriend. Right?"

"Right. But I want you to know that no matter what happens you are still the most important thing in my life. That won't change, okay?"

"Okay."

"And there are times when Jackson might sleep here. This is your house too, so I want to know if you are okay with that."

"Will you let him play *Dragon Master* before bed?"

"Only if you two are being good," I reply.

"Yay! When is he coming over? Is he sleeping here tonight? Can I wait up for him? Can you make him a shark outfit for Halloween too?"

"Maybe. I'll ask him what he wants to be for Halloween. Just tell me this: are you sure you are okay with us adding someone else to our home?"

"Yup! Are you sure Dad won't be mad at me?"

"Yup!" I reply.

"Okay. Night, Mom."

"Good night, honey."

Jackson is working late, but since we haven't spent time together this week, he wants to come and say hi before he goes home. I could tell by the tone in his voice that he has something on his mind. It could be that he is waiting to hear me say "I love you," or it could be the fact that we haven't been intimate yet.

Argo was wondering the same thing too. In fact, he kept texting me pictures of blue balls all day. It would literally be a picture of a blue basketball or a blue soccer ball. And finally, my ever so subtle best friend sent me a picture of a vervet monkey squatting in the forest with its legs open. I accused Argo of altering the picture and coloring the monkey's balls blue. He then sent me a link to Wikipedia; as it turns out, the vervet monkey's balls are naturally blue.

That damn picture made my day. But the one who is about to make my night is Jackson. And he has just knocked on the door. I rush to open it and wrap my arms around his neck. He holds me close. We kiss. It's so good to have his lips on mine. I let him in and close the door behind him.

We continue to make out for a while. What Jackson's touch does to my body is criminal. We've made out before, but there's hunger in the way he's kissing me right now. There's a carnal need in the way his tongue ensnares mine. Suddenly, I see that stupid monkey in my mind's eye. I giggle and rest my head on his chest.

"What's so funny?" he asks.

"Nothing, just remind me to kill Argo when I see him tomorrow," I reply.

"Done," he says. "Is Aaron asleep already?"

"Yeah, you just missed him." His reaction is slight, but I catch it—he's disappointed. That really touches me. The fact that seeing my son makes a difference in his day…that means the world.

"Did he pick out his Halloween costume yet?" Jackson asks.

"Oh, you know about that?"

"Yeah, I put in a vote for the hammerhead. Please tell me that it's still in the running."

"Yup, it's still on the ballot."

"Yes!" He laughs.

"Are you hungry? Can I make you a sandwich?"

"Sure," he says as he follows me to the kitchen. I can feel him watching my ass move. And I may or may not have walked particularly slowly so that he could get a nice view.

I take out the deli meats and cheeses. Jackson gets the plates, opens a beer for himself, and pours a glass of red wine for me. I don't drink beer, but he does, and so I got him the kind he likes. Argo says keeping something in your home because the person you're with likes it is more of a sign of commitment than a marriage proposal.

I make two turkey and Swiss cheese sandwiches and bring them over to the dinner table. Jackson brings in the drinks. He eats his sandwich in a few big bites. I ask if he wants another and he says he's fine for now. I take a bite of my food and sip the wine. We sit in silence for a few moments, but there's definitely something in the air.

"Is everything okay?" I ask.

He takes a deep breath and pushes his plate away. "I was going to ask you that actually," he admits.

"What do you mean?"

"Well, ever since I said I love you, you've been hard to get in touch with," he says.

"I'm sorry. I'm not avoiding you."

He tilts his head slightly. I catch a flash of sadness on his face, but it fades so quickly, I'm not sure that's what I really saw. I get up and sit on his lap. That move surprises him. I wrap my arms around his neck as he gazes at me.

"Hi," I say simply.

"Hello," he says, looking down at me.

"I know you…" I tease.

"Yeah, I'm the guy who poured your wine." He smiles.

"No, that's not how I know you. Oh wait; you're the guy I'm in love with."

"I am?" he says with such tenderness, it makes my heart flutter.

"Yes, you are," I reply as I lean in and kiss him. The more time passes, the deeper we kiss. It's to the point where I can feel his erection. And judging by the bulge I feel under me, Jackson Hunter is going to make me one happy woman. He starts kissing down my neck, while his large hands fondle my breasts through my shirt. It's a hint of what's to come, and dear God I want it.

Jackson clears his throat and pulls away. "Baby, we have to stop."

"Maybe we don't. I started taking the pill a few days ago. And I talked to Aaron about us, and he loves you. He loves us being together. I think it's okay if you stay over," I reply as I kiss his neck. He sighs reluctantly and puts distance between us.

"What is it?" I ask, getting worried.

"I'm glad Aaron is okay with us. And baby, I love that kid too."

"Why do I hear a 'but' coming?"

"*However*, I have to be at work at 4 AM. That only gives us three hours. And I don't want our first time to be rushed. You deserve better than that. And I actually came here to talk to you about something."

"Okay, what's up?" I ask.

"First, you should probably get off my lap. I can't think when you're so close, baby. It's hard—literally."

Monkeys.

DAMN YOU, ARGO!

I get back to my own seat, and he laughs. "Sorry, you are really fucking distracting, and I can't wait to take you to bed. You have no idea how much I want you," he says. I blush and avert my eyes.

"Here's the thing I wanted to tell you: All my brothers married amazing women. You'll meet most of them at dinner this weekend. The thing is that while their relationships are strong and happy, it almost didn't happen for them."

"What do you mean? Why not?"

"Wyatt's wife, Winter, and Cash's wife, Skylar, had trust issues. And they were right to have that. They went through a lot in their lives. But they almost lost out on their marriage and their happiness because they hid things from their mates."

"What things?"

"Things that they should have been sharing with their partners, but instead, they hid. They didn't do it to be malicious, but in the end, it didn't matter. The lying and the secrecy almost ended their marriage before it started. My sister-in-law Shay hid something from my brother

Logan. She was going through some stuff, and she was determined to fix it by herself. She sent him away. And that cost them three years that they will never get back."

"Are they okay now?" I ask.

"Yeah, they are, but only because they were able to sort it out. Baby, I don't want us to have a misunderstanding like that. I want you to feel like you can tell me anything, because you can."

"You think I'm keeping something from you?" I ask over the pounding of my heart.

"I don't know, are you?"

I look down but don't reply. "Mia, whatever is going on, I won't judge you. But you have to talk to me."

I get up and start pacing the room. "What makes you think something is going on?" I ask.

"I get paid to observe things. It's not hard to see that something is different with you. There's also the fact that you changed your number and you added more security, and while I'm a fan of that, there's usually a reason," he says as he gets up and stands in front of me.

"It was a little thing, but I think I handled it."

"Does it have to do with a client? Is that it? Did a client threaten you?"

"No client threatened me. I promise."

"Okay, so this is all just you being more careful?"

"Yes."

"And nothing prompted it?"

"No…"

"Okay, well I'm glad you upped your system. I want you and Aaron to be safe," he says as he pulls me to him. Our lips collide in a series of breathless, smoldering kisses.

I want to enjoy this moment. I want to take in Jackson's masculine scent and the feel of his strong arms around me. But can't; I'm too busy with taking in the gut-twisting truth: I just lied to the man I love.

Chapter 13

Jackson

I know my girl is hiding something. I know it the same way I knew that there was something in Skull's file that I was overlooking. It's a gut feeling, and I always trust my gut. The fact is, sometimes that's all a cop has. If I were working a case, I'd know exactly what to do. But since this is a personal issue, I have no fucking idea what I'm supposed to do next.

If I push the issue, then she'll feel like I don't trust her. If I let it go, it could come back to bite us in the ass. Now, if it does, and it's a little sting, okay. But if it's something that's gonna take a big chunk of flesh from our asses, then I want to know about it now.

It's not just my gut that tells me something is off. There's more to it than that. It's the way she's been acting lately. She's been jumpy and nervous. She double-checks her locks and holds her breath when her cell rings, and her shoulders only relax once she sees it's me at the door. What the hell is that about?

I'm no mental health expert, but I know people. And I know that they don't just wake up one day and change their behavior. In order for that to happen, there has to be some kind of trigger. A guy who's been living on burgers and fries for twenty years doesn't just wake up and decide to eat a salad. It's experiencing slight chest pain, or worse, a heart attack, which forced him to change.

I could find out if I really wanted to, I know that. I have more than enough access to figure out what's happening. But if I do that, then that makes me the douchebag who invaded her privacy. And what's more, I need to know that she feels close enough to me to tell me. I want to be involved in her life. But how can that happen when she won't talk to me?

I down my first and last beer. I don't want to get drunk. I want some clarity. I thought I would be able to get it from Mia, but so far, nothing. I place the bottle on the bar and pay my tab. I'm about to head out and go home, but then I reconsider. I need answers, and home isn't going to give them to me.

So, instead, I find myself driving over to my brother Logan's house. He and his wife, Shay, had major trust issues. Like I told Mia, Shay had her reasons, but in the end, it was a hard road because she hid things from him.

I'm going over there because I need someone to say this stuff to and also because I want to steal whatever leftovers they have from dinner at Wyatt's house last night. Wyatt is almost as good in the kitchen as he is in the field. So, naturally, when he makes dinner, we all line up to eat and sometimes steal from each other.

I pull up to the driveway and then knock on the door. Logan comes out. He's not as handsome as I am, although there's a rumor he might not be utterly hideous. Okay, okay, most women I know say he's hot. Whatever.

"Fuck you want?" Logan says.

"A brother with better manners, for one," I counter.

"Wrong house. You're looking for Wyatt."

"Fuck you!" I reply with a grin.

"Get the hell in here," he says as he steps aside to let me in. I see Shay coming towards me with their baby, Miles. He has his mom's wild, dark good looks. He giggles when he sees me. I greet Shay and pick my nephew up.

"Hey, put my kid down. I don't want him growing up thinking the FBI is a worthwhile place to work," Logan says.

"Don't listen to my husband. You hold him as long as you want," Shay says.

"I promise I will come back and babysit, but right now, I really need to talk to you," I reply.

"To Shay or me?" Logan asks.

"What the hell would I want with you? When is SWAT ever useful?" I tease.

"Fuck off," he replies. I laugh and hand Miles back to him.

"Seriously, I came to talk to Shay. The smart one in the house," I counter.

"Oh really? Get the fuck out! Right now."

"Yeah, like you could take me," I reply.

"Any day, old man," he counters.

"Logan, take Miles upstairs while I talk to Jackson."

"What do you have to eat?" I ask.

"Don't feed him; he'll never fucking leave!" Logan says as he goes up the stairs with his son in his arms.

"You love having me. I make your life interesting," I shout back.

"Shay, don't you give him any leftovers from Wyatt's. I'm gonna eat that tomorrow. Put a padlock on the pasta. Greedy bastard," he says from the top of the stairs.

I follow Shay into her kitchen, and right away I begin to swipe all the good stuff from Wyatt's dinner. I pile on the food, but I'm sure I'm gonna have to take it to go—my heart's not in it right now.

"Everything okay, Jackson?"

"No. What the hell is wrong with you women?" I ask before I can stop myself.

She puts her hands on her hips and says, "Not a damn thing."

I smile at her. I do like her. She doesn't take any shit from anyone. Not even her pushy brother-in-law who raids her fridge and demands to talk to her. "I'm being a dick, right?" I ask.

"Yeah, kind of. But that's okay. You've got a little credit left with me. I saw the raid—good job on the takedown. But seriously, did you call Wyatt for a flesh wound?" she teases.

"He was around the area, and the hospital did that," I argue.

"Yeah, well you know the rules—"

"Yeah, I know. Only internal bleeding or actual death calls for getting the family together."

"That or Wyatt's food."

"Yeah, that too," I reply.

"Okay, so what's wrong? Is it this new girl you're seeing?"

"Her name is Mia."

"Well, we don't really know what her name is—Shelby hasn't given her one yet," she jokes. I roll my eyes. My sister-in-law has a nickname for all the women we marry.

"Well as of now, her name is Mia."

"Okay, deal. So tell me about Mia."

I tell her the basics and why I'm frustrated. "I mean, I know she's hiding something but why doesn't she just come out and tell me? You kept secrets from Logan, why did you do it?"

"I wanted to protect him. And just to be clear, our situation was not the same as yours."

"Why not? Mia is hiding something from me."

"No, you're hiding things from each other. Logan never hid anything from me. I did all the hiding because I thought it was what was best. I was wrong. And yes, Mia is wrong here because she needs to trust you and open up. But she's not the only one who is wrong here."

"What did I do?"

"Winter told me you can't sleep. That usually has to do with work. Did you tell her about that?"

"Well...no."

"Okay, and did you tell her about what Agent Green's fiancée asked you to do and why you said no, and how that ended up?"

"No, I can't tell her any of that."

"Well, then help me out here, Jackson. How do you expect a woman to let you in when all you do is keep her out?"

"Ouch," I grumble.

She laughs and says, "Yeah, you should have gone to Winter's house. She's much nicer."

Although Shay's blunt, she's also sincere in trying to help me. I give her a quick hug and thank her.

"Hey, get off my woman," Logan says, appearing behind us.

"You really picked the wrong brother," I remark to Shay. She laughs. Logan spots the food on the counter and tries to take it back. And yes, we do fight over the food.

Mia

The thing about being stalked is you can lose all sense of what's real and what's just in your head. I was at the market, and I could have sworn there was a figure looming just a few yards from me. I could feel the person marking my every move, mirroring my every turn. So, I turned around to confront him, but he was gone. It could have been my mind playing tricks on me.

The day before that, I heard footsteps coming towards me in the parking lot of a department store, and I started running. The person began to run faster and faster. I quickly took out my mace and prepared to spray, only to find that it was the store security—I'd dropped my parking validation.

And then there was this morning, when I damn near electrocuted a cat because it was lurking in the bushes just outside my apartment. I called Officer Peterson, and he updated me by telling me there was no update. He said they are looking for Gorman but can't seem to find him anywhere. He is keeping a low profile. The officer told me to sit tight and said maybe Gorman got sick of coming after me and took off. I could have explained to him all the reasons why that wasn't likely, but I decided it wasn't worth it.

I only leave the office building with building security, and I have given up on going out in the evening unless it's in a group or with

Jackson. That's why I'm relieved when he calls and makes plans for tonight.

He wants us to have dinner alone before I meet his family. I was going to decline because my sitter couldn't make it, but Argo wouldn't hear of it. So, he's spending Saturday night watching Aaron for me. I'm not sure what they have planned, but I am sure that something will be sparkled in my home that wasn't sparkled previously.

Jackson picks me up at home and greets Aaron. The two of them had their own thing earlier. He took Aaron to the arcade after his homework was done. They had lunch at the restaurant connected to the arcade. Jackson swears that they didn't overdo the junk food, but I'm pretty sure both of them were on a sugar high when they got back.

Jackson then greets Argo; soon Argo is kicking us out the door. Jackson won't tell me where he's taking me, says it's a surprise. He walks me out to the front, where a car and driver await.

"Wow, our very own chauffeur?" I ask.

"I'm trying to impress you. Is it working?" he teases.

"I will let you know." I smile back. The car takes us to Fourth Street in lower Manhattan. When we get out, I look up and see the restaurant I told him I was dying to try: One if by Land, Two if by Sea. I told him I was in love with their tasting menu; I saw it online and tried to get a reservation, but they were always booked.

I don't particularly care for fancy, pretentious places, but this place has incredible food, an extensive wine list, and elegant, romantic décor. I told Jackson looking at pictures of their dining area actually made me regret being single—something I rarely felt. Before I met Jackson, I promised myself I would one day work up the nerve to go there alone—if the reservation list ever opened up.

"You remembered?" I ask.

"It's something you wanted to try, and I want to be the one you try it with if that's okay," he says.

"Yes, that's better than okay. Thank you," I reply, getting on the tips of my toes to kiss Jackson. We enter the red door and are greeted with the scent of the freshly polished wooden staircase. The dining area has dark hardwood floors, and gleaming crystal chandeliers hang overhead.

The tables are decorated with crisp, stark-white tablecloths, candles, and elegant stemware. The focal point of the room is the brick fireplace and the baby grand piano. It's only missing one thing.

"Where are the other patrons? Why is it just us?" I ask.

"I didn't feel like sharing you tonight."

"What? Wait, this is all just for us?"

"For you, baby; this is all for you," he says just as we are shown to our table—which is basically every table. We are seated on the balcony that looks out onto the magnificent garden below.

"This is wonderful, but you didn't have to do this," I assure him.

"I know. I also know that I could take you to a dollar menu drive-through and you'd still be as gracious as you are in this place. That's a hard thing to find in someone. I'm a lucky guy."

"Well, Agent Hunter, color me impressed and smitten."

We go on to have the most delightful meal I've had in a very long time. We chose the tasting menu, and each course was paired with a different wine. It was a seven-course meal, and by the end, I'm stuffed and happy. I thank him again for such a great dinner.

"I'm just happy we're here together. Mia, someone pointed out to me the other day that I was asking you to open up, but all the while I was closed off. Well, I want that to change tonight. I'll tell you something I've been trying to hide from, and I'm hoping it will help you turn to me—should you need the help."

"This sounds serious," I mumble.

"It is. I've never talked about it to anyone who wasn't in my family."

"Jackson, what is it?"

"There's this woman, her name is Megan, and I killed her fiancé."

Chapter 14

Jackson

I was supposed to start speaking and tell her everything. But nothing came out. She placed her hand on top of mine and suggested we go to my place. She thought I'd be more at ease. She was right. The moment we got to my place and settled in on the sofa, I felt better. I felt like I could say the things I needed to say.

"You knew changing the atmosphere would work, didn't you?" I ask.

"It was worth a shot. Are you sure you're up to talking?"

"Yeah, I am. I want us to be the kind of couple who actually talks about real shit," I reply. She blushes and averts her eyes.

"What is it?"

"I've never heard you call us a couple before. I like the sound of that," she admits.

"Yeah, me too. I've been single forever and it never even occurred to me to mind it. It was all about one-night stands here and there. It shocked the hell out of me that I wanted more with you—with anyone."

"Same here. I haven't bought a virtual cat in weeks," she jokes.

"Argo will be very impressed."

"Speaking of which, let me just check in with him for a minute. I want to make sure Aaron doesn't talk him into anything crazy."

"You think Argo would get played by a seven-year-old?"

"Last year, I was out of town for a conference; I came back two days later to find Argo and Aaron hiding under the bed. My son had convinced Argo to watch a slasher movie marathon. Aaron was so freaked out I had to coax him out from under the bed with a pack of M&Ms."

"And what did you use to get Argo out from under the bed?" I laugh.

"Coupons for MAC cosmetics," she says with a big grin. I wait as she checks up on Aaron. Argo tells her that he's been asleep for a while and that she can sleep over if she wants. He's settled in for the night.

"So, what do you think? Is it okay if I stay over?" she asks.

"A gorgeous woman in my home, who loves me and wants to have sex with me? God, that sounds awful." I smile.

"Then it's settled," she says as she hangs up the phone. "Now, talk to me; who is Megan and what happened to her fiancé?"

"His name was Robert Green; he was an agent. As you know, there are different departments that make up the FBI. Agent Green was an analyst. He sorted through a multitude of data and was among the best when it came to information gathering. He hated it. His dream was to be out in the field. Every chance he got, he was training and working his ass off to qualify for fieldwork.

"When it came down to it, no matter how prepared he was in other areas, he'd always choke on his firearms requirement. He'd get nervous, forget to breathe, and basically lose it. His hands got so sweaty that once he actually allowed a gun to slip from his fingers. He almost shot himself. He became kind of a running joke in the department. Guys would say things like, 'Don't Green the situation.'

"I felt bad for him, but I knew that not everyone was meant to carry a gun. He asked for my help, and I pointed out that there was more than one way to be of service. But he wanted field action, and I could see he would never stop until he got what he wanted.

"One day, we got some bad info, and had it not been for Green we would have walked right into a trap and gotten our asses handed to us. A few days later, I was at the gun range, and I saw him. I went over to thank him for saving our op, and we started talking. He was a very well-rounded guy. He understood more than just data. He had an insight into human nature and a keen sense of his surroundings. Those skills are imperative for an FBI agent in the field.

"I stayed behind and watched him handle his gun. He was awful at it, but not hopeless. I gave him a few pointers. It took a few days, but soon his aim had improved. I learned to shoot from different people, my dad being the first. But the person who had the most impact while teaching me was my brother Cash; he's never missed his target. He gave me pointers on how to work with Green.

"I drilled him hard, and he never once complained. It took weeks to get him anywhere near ready to reattempt his firearms test. We got closer as he trained. I learned that he was about to marry his high school sweetheart, Megan. The two of them were about to have their first baby. They were looking forward to moving out of her mom's house and starting a new life together. Mia, I really liked the guy. He had integrity, and he genuinely gave a damn about helping people.

"He invited me over to dinner to meet his fiancée and the rest of his family. I went, and I had a great time. Megan was funny, loud, and silly, a really nice girl. Just after dessert, Megan offered to take me on a tour of the house. She did that so we could be alone. And once we were, she asked me for a favor."

"What did she want?"

I can feel the memories of that night flooding my body. My chest tightens, and my shoulders tense up. I know how this story ends, and telling it doesn't change that. But I keep going; it's too late to turn back now. And Mia is worth it. I want to be open with her.

"Megan asked me how Green's training was going. She said that he was positive that he would pass this time. I told her that he was right. We had been doing drills that were above and beyond what the department required. There was no doubt in my mind he'd pass. We even drilled under stressful situations where Green was on a timer and had to hit a moving target.

"She said, 'If that's the case, I need a favor. I need you to reject his transfer to active duty.' She went on to tell me how terrified she was that something would happen to him in the field. Every time he failed his test, she secretly breathed a sigh of relief because she hated the thought of his getting hurt. But since he was always failing his test, she thought she had nothing to worry about."

"And then you started training him, and she got nervous," Mia reasons.

"Yeah, she heard how well he was doing. She started to freak out at the thought that he'd soon carry a gun and go into danger. So, she asked me to sabotage him so that he would stay safe at a desk job."

"Jackson, do you have that kind of pull with your bosses?"

"Unofficially, yes. It's rare to lead a team at my age. Teams are usually run by guys seven to ten years older than me. And because I do head the team, if I rejected Green, he wouldn't have gotten very far. Megan knew that. She knew that if I voiced any objection to Green joining us, it wouldn't matter what his firearms test results were, he'd never be chosen for field work."

"What did you tell her?"

"I said no. I told her that he had worked hard and that she should talk to him about her fears if she felt that strongly about it. She said she'd talked to him, but he wouldn't listen. This was his dream, and he couldn't let it go."

"I take it she didn't let it go either?" Mia says.

I laugh bitterly. "No, not a chance. She kept calling and coming by the office. She said she had a bad feeling about him being in the field and that it was my duty as his friend to protect him from himself. She came to me, Mia, sobbing, pregnant, and desperate. She begged me, 'Don't let him get the promotion. Do this for our baby. It's a girl. Her name is Willa. Please don't let her grow up without a dad.'" My voice fades. I hang my head between my hands and massage my temples.

"Jackson, what happened? You can tell me," she says as she rests her forehead on my arm and patiently waits. I get up and walk towards the window. There's very little room in the house with all the space my guilt is taking up.

"No matter how much she begged, I said no. When the time came to take his test, he aced it. He was so damn happy, baby. He actually danced his way out of the gun range. He wanted to go out for drinks and celebrate. So we did. The whole time Megan was looking over at me with dread in her eyes. She tried one last time to get me to reject him, but when the time came, I approved his transfer.

"Two weeks later, we got a tip about a terrorist cell that had been activated. They were planning an attack in the heart of midtown, using suicide bombers. We were dispatched immediately, and out of the nine bombers, we stopped eight of them. But the last one had gotten away. When I caught up with her, she turned to face me. That's when I saw her eyes—she had Rose's eyes.

"I begged her to surrender and put her hands up, but she wouldn't. When she went to arm the bomb, I tried to talk her down. But I was lying to myself. The girl could not be talked out of it. She set the bomb off and took two members of my team, including Green.

"His body was shredded. They didn't even have enough of him left to have an open casket. I saw Megan at the funeral, and she was in such bad shape she had to be taken to the ER. That was my fault."

"No, Jackson, you didn't do anything wrong," she pleads as she comes closer.

"Mia, I could have saved him. I could have done what she asked me to do and rejected him. He'd still be here, taking Megan to get checkups and preparing for his first kid to arrive. Instead, he's gone, and some poor baby will never lay eyes on her dad. Why didn't I just…" My voice dies in my throat.

"Why didn't you just lie and say Green wasn't field ready? Because that's not who you are. And because that's what he wanted. We don't get to choose how we die, Jackson, just how we live. And he wanted this to be his life. You are not to blame. You felt he was ready. The department felt he was ready, and most of all, Green himself felt that he was ready.

"You can't let this eat away at you. It's a sad thing that happened. But I have news for you, Agent Hunter; it's not your job to stop every bad thing from happening. Honey, you're just one man, that's it. You go out there and do what you can. The rest is out of your hands. And you need to know that, or you're in for a very rough ride."

"Mia…he was so happy to make the team. I can still see his face in my head. He was on top of the world."

"Yes, and you gave that to him. You helped him make his dream become a reality. And when that kid grows up, she'll know that her dad was fearless, and determined in pursuing his dreams. That's the stock she comes from. One day, Megan and her daughter will stop grieving and look at the legacy Green left behind and not the pain of his absence. It just takes time," she says as she takes my hand in hers.

"You really believe that?"

"Yes, I really do."

"I can't sleep. I try but…"

"Hey," she says softly as she gets up on her toes and gives me a quick kiss. "Jackson, you can't save everyone. And if you don't take care of yourself, you can't help save *anyone*."

She's right; I know that. It's just that I never thought of it that way. Green was happy in the end. He had this inner glow. He died, yes. But he did so doing the thing that made him feel most alive.

"God, you're amazing!" I reply as I wrap my arms around her.

"See, you missed out on a great therapist," she teases.

"That's okay; I got an even better deal: a super-hot girlfriend who is easy to talk to and very easy to love."

"Well, just so you know, I'm billing you for my services."

"Oh, I see. This isn't a freebie?"

"Nope. Pay up." We laugh, and I gaze into her eyes, those beautiful eyes that seem to haunt me at times. That gets me back to the reason I started this. "Mia, something is wrong. I can tell. Please tell me, what's going on with you, baby?"

Mia

For the record, I was going to tell Jackson right then and there. But then he got a call from work, and they needed him to go in right away. He couldn't tell me exactly what was going on, but I could tell by his tone it was urgent. He got his gun and his jacket and headed towards the door. Before he left, he made me promise to stay here and wait for him.

"We are not done. You're not getting out of talking to me. Stay, get some rest, I'll be back as soon as I can. I love you," he said, followed by a quick kiss.

"I love you too. Please be careful. And remember—I hate heroes. Don't be one," I replied, only partly joking.

"Promise," he said as he took off.

I have mixed feelings about what just happened. On the one hand, I'm glad to spare Jackson my drama for yet a few more hours. But on the other hand, it would be good to come clean. Maybe Argo was right, and I should have told him in the first place. Okay, I can't change not telling him, but I can try and fix it. I sat on the sofa and turned on the TV, thinking I'd wait up for Jackson but I dozed off.

It's morning now, and sunlight is streaming through the windows. I text Argo and ask if everything is okay. He texts me back, saying, "6 AM on a Sunday, let me and the boy sleep. Go take a ride on the Hunter train and don't get off until he gets off." I shake my head and laugh at his text.

"Wow, that laugh must drive Jackson crazy with lust. Good for you, Mona Lisa," someone says from the corner of the room. I nearly jump out of my skin. I leap off the sofa, turn, and find a beautiful, impeccably dressed black woman standing in the corner. She's dressed in high-end designer garb from head to toe. She's the kind of woman that has daily manicures and spa treatments. Her skin glows, and her makeup is immaculate.

"Who the hell are you? And how did you get in here?!" I demand.

"I'm Shelby—Jackson's sister-in-law. I married the first brother, the CIA guy," she says proudly.

"Are you supposed to be telling me that?"

"Well, we'll most likely be family someday, so…"

"What are you talking about?"

"I have a talent for spotting the women the brothers will marry. And you, Mona Lisa, fit the bill. You're hot-tempered, you do charity work, and you have a great ass. So again, good for you! Now coffee, how do you take it?"

"Okay, I'm not sure what's really going on here but—wait, how did you get in here?"

She tilts her head back and laughs. "Please. I'm Shelby."

"Is that supposed to mean something?"

"I have keys to, well, everything. It's just my way."

"Your way is breaking into people's homes?"

"Sometimes. It depends on my mood."

"Okay, you're nuts."

"Well, a little insanity might help you in this family. Things can get crazy. The long hours, the cases, the stakeouts, the bullets, and anyway, I thought I'd take a look at Jackson's very own Mona Lisa. And you know what? I approve."

"Um, thanks. Why do you keep calling me Mona Lisa? My name is Mia."

"Is it?" she says with a knowing smile. She goes to the kitchen to make me coffee.

"I don't want any, thank you. Maybe you should come back when Jackson is here," I offer.

"Mona Lisa, you and I should get to know each other."

"And why is that? And again, my name is not Mona Lisa!" I counter.

She sits at the kitchen table and signals for me to sit next to her. This lady is crazy. But I do as she asks.

"First off, congrats on landing Jackson, he's a very high-quality find. A few things you should know: I've talked to some of the women he's hooked up with, and well, make sure you stretch and hydrate."

"Oh my God," I reply as I bury my face in my hands.

"The other thing you need to know is that you will need to develop a 'don't try me' stare to ward off all these women trying to claim him. And there are many. Hell, if I wasn't married... He's got that searing alpha stare but balances it with his witty charm. Again, good for you!"

"Are you usually like this?" I ask.

"No, sometimes I can be intrusive."

Seriously?

"Look, I meant to see you earlier, but to be honest, I was having a hard time getting the info I needed on you."

"Info? Your family is checking up on me?"

"Come now, the Hunters are worth half a billion dollars. Do you think they wouldn't have background checks?"

"So, Jackson is having someone spy on me?"

"Oh please, men know nothing. His mom is having you looked into. She does it to all the women her boys are into—don't take it personally."

"What? This is crazy! What kind of family does that?"

"Oh, so you'd let Aaron just walk in the house with any girl and not ask questions?"

"How do you know about—never mind," I sigh.

She laughs. "I think we are starting to get each other."

"I don't know about that," I reply. She gets up and noses around the room. "If there's nothing else, I'll tell Jackson you came by, Shelby."

She heads towards the window and speaks in a light voice as if she's whispering something that should never be said out loud. "Did you know that Mona Lisa wasn't her real name?"

"Um no, I didn't."

"Her real name was Lisa Gherardini. She was painted in 1503. The painting appears massive, but it's actually kind of small, fragile. She sits in her own room in the Louvre, in a climate-controlled space; she sits in the prettiest prison in the world. She's been attacked, she's been scarred, and since she was created, she's been hunted by men who thought they owned her…"

My throat goes dry, and my voice barely makes it out of my mouth. "Are you saying that's me?"

"You don't exist online. There's the handle of what appears to be a Taser sticking out of your handbag. And when you turned around and saw I was here, you weren't scared of me; you were relieved to know it wasn't the person you thought it would be. You were expecting someone else. Someone you fear. I know that look very well."

I ask her pointedly, "Why do you know the look of fear so well?"

"For years, it was the only expression I ever wore," she says, lost in thought.

"Shelby…"

She turns back to look at me. She's smiling and engaging like she was when I first laid eyes on her. The soft-spoken woman is gone. "I have to go. I don't know what Dr. Mia Samuels is up to, but I do know that Mia Avery needs to be honest with Jackson. Because if you are in as much trouble as I think you are, you'll need him. In fact, you'll need all five of the brothers."

Chapter 15

Mia

I'm in Aaron's room fighting a battle with his unruly hair, and his hair is winning. It takes almost twenty minutes to get his curls somewhat under control. He hates me playing with his hair and complains the whole time. When I'm done, he quickly runs out of the room fearing I may call him back to torment him some more.

"We're leaving in half an hour. Don't get your clothes dirty, Aaron. I mean it!" I shout.

"Girl, leave him alone. Jackson's family will love him. He's seven. Cute is built in. The person who has to worry about impressing his family is you," Argo teases from the doorway.

"Well, I'm sure that's already blown since Shelby probably told everyone my real name."

"Well, they didn't cancel on you, that means they are still interested. And most importantly so is Jackson."

"Yeah, he's a really good guy," I reply sadly. Argo goes over to the bar cart in the living room and pours us each a glass of red wine. I sip it as I get lost in thought.

"What is it?" Argo asks.

"I'm planning to talk to Jackson tonight after the dinner, but I can't help but feel awful about dropping this whole thing in his lap."

"It's not your fault this is happening. He will understand, and you two will face it together. So stop worrying."

"You're right. We will go to his parents' place, have a nice dinner, and then talk afterward. Everything will be fine."

"Okay, now say that again, but this time, do it without your hands shaking," Argo instructs. I take a big gulp of my wine, and Argo takes it away from me. "Drunk while meeting his parents is trashy and basic. We are better than that."

"Okay, you're right again." I walk over to the mirror and look myself over. I take a deep breath and ask, "How do I look?"

Argo will be the first to tell me if what I'm wearing does or does not work. I picked out a simple yet elegant emerald green pencil dress. I matched it with my favorite pair of heels and diamond stud earrings. I put on eyeliner and lip gloss with a hint of color.

"Yes, you are all of that!" Argo says, looking me over. He puts a strand of stray hair back in place and smiles. "Enjoy this, okay, Mimi? Don't go all nuts on me. Be easy and relaxed. Jackson is lucky to have you, and he knows that."

"Thank you. Now what about you, what's going on with you and your dad?"

He rolls his eyes and sighs heavily.

"Uh-oh. That can't be good. What happened?" I ask.

"So, we've been talking, right? And so far, it's been really nice and everything. But then the other day, he asked if I was seeing someone. I said no. And he seemed kind of relieved. Like maybe I was taking a break from being gay. Is that it? Does he think me being gay is a phase? Cuz, um…no!"

"Argo, I'm sorry he reacted that way, but give him a chance. You two are trying. That's what's important."

"Yeah, but what if he never accepts me?"

"He wants you in his life; otherwise, he would break off contact. The thing about parents is that they have our lives planned out for us. Your dad had a picture in his head of how your life would look: Argo will be married, he will have kids, and he will have a good paying job and be happy. When he learned that you are gay, that picture faded."

"Just because I'm gay doesn't mean I can't have those things."

"I agree, but he doesn't know that yet. For him, he's watching the picture in his head burn right through. But when he gets to know you, as an adult, he'll see that there's a new picture. And in that picture you are still married, still have kids and a good job. But the only difference is there's a man next to you instead of a woman.

"It's a big adjustment for him to make. But don't give up on him. So long as he's willing to call and talk, you be there on the other end. He won't be able to resist letting you back into his heart, how could he? You're amazing!"

Argo looks at his reflection in the mirror. "I want to argue, but you're right, I'm freaking adorable. I mean like Blue Ivy adorable."

We laugh just as Aaron runs into the room. "Mom, remember you said not to get dirty?"

"Yes…"

"Is ketchup dirty?"

ARGH!

Jackson wanted to pick us up, but I told him we were fine to drive. I rarely use my car because the trains are faster during rush hour. But I love driving, and since it's Sunday evening, the traffic is pretty light. Also, Jackson would have had to come all the way to the other end of town to come to get us and go back up to his parents' place. It didn't make sense. I explained all that to him, and he still argued with me. I promised him if he let me drive my car over there, we could make out in the back seat. He agreed.

Another reason I wanted to drive was so that I could get my bearings. It's been years since I had to meet a man's family. Tom's mom was nice and very welcoming, but I can't recall what I said or did to make her like me. I'm out of practice. Driving here on my own allows me to take one last moment for myself. And boy do I need it.

When I pull up into the driveway, my mouth drops. I figured the house would be big, but I wasn't expecting an actual mansion.

"Mom, that house is super big!" Aaron says.

"Yeah, it really is."

"It looks like a rapper's house. Jackson's mom and dad live there?"

"Yeah," I reply, feeling somewhat overwhelmed. The house boasts large columns, a circular driveway, and a vast, well-manicured lawn. It looks like something out of *Architectural Digest*. My hands are suddenly cold and clammy. I swallow hard and try to keep my anxiety at bay. I just need a few minutes before I enter; yeah, just a few more minutes.

Five minutes pass.

Just a little while longer.

"Mom, I have to pee." I look at Aaron in the rearview mirror and promise him we'll get out in a second. And then my mind drifts. What if they don't like us? What if I don't like them? What happens when they find out about my past? Will they warn Jackson to stay away? Can I really blame them? And if that's the case, what happens if this thing doesn't work out? How will I break the news to Aaron?

"Mom!"

I hear Aaron, but my doubts somewhat mute his voice. I keep hearing the same thoughts over and over again in my head. This entire thing might be pointless. Shelby could have told everyone she suspects that I'm a liar and that I have a dark past. Why didn't they cancel tonight? What are they planning? What the hell am I walking into?

"Jackson!" Aaron shouts.

I was too in my head to notice that Jackson has come out of the mansion and is now standing by the car, looking in. Aaron pounds excitedly on the car window; I unlock the car door. Aaron unbuckles his seatbelt, gets out of the car, and hops up and down. He looks up at Jackson with a pleading expression; Jackson laughs and says, "Through the front door, make a right."

"Thanks!" Aaron says as he takes off into the house. I'm still somewhat stuck with my hands gripping the steering wheel. Much to my surprise, he doesn't tell me to get out of the car; instead, he gets in the back seat and lies flat on his back.

"What are you doing?" I ask as I look at him in the rearview mirror.

"I need a quick session, Doc. It's important," he says.

"Oh, so this is a session?"

"Yup. Here's my problem. I'm hopelessly in love with this stunning redhead and her awesome kid. But she somehow managed to glue herself to her car. It's that super glue, the kind that just won't come off. So, how do I get her unstuck from the steering wheel?"

"You could love her despite what she's attached to," I reply.

"I don't know, Doc. What would become of your sex life? Car sex is the number one cause of sex-related injuries. I'd be taking my life in my hands."

"Then you have to get her 'unstuck,'" I reply with a silly grin.

"How?"

I think for a moment. Suddenly, I find myself no longer being playful. "Tell her that no matter what happens inside that house, it won't change the way you feel about her. Tell her this thing between you two is real."

He sits up, no longer joking. His eyes are dark and serious. I take off my seatbelt and turn to the back seat, facing him.

"Mia, there isn't a goddamn thing that can make me stop loving you and Aaron. My family will love you, just as I do. But even if by some small chance they don't, it would not change anything between us. Do you hear me? Not one damn thing. You and Aaron are more than my 'right now.' You two are my future. If you want to blow tonight off, get some pizza, and watch a movie, then let's go and do that.

"If you want to spend the night with Aaron, bowling badly and eating junk food, I'm good with that too. I don't care where we go or what we do, as long as I get to do it with the two of you.

"But if I get a vote, I'd love for you to come inside. I want them to meet the reason why I'm happy. I want them to meet the best thing that's ever happened to me."

I place my hands behind his head, bring him close to my face, and claim him with a long, ardent kiss.

Someone knocks on the window. "Mom, let's go! They got grilled cheese! And you know what it's shaped like?!"

Jackson and I reply in unison, "Sharks."

"YES!"

We laugh and get out of the car. Jackson takes in my outfit and whispers in my ear, "You look beautiful, baby." I beam. Aaron eagerly takes my hand and guides me into the house.

The inside is even more impressive than the outside if that's possible. The marble floors, crown molding, and large-scale art make the home almost too picturesque to be real. The foyer has an exquisite bouquet of fresh flowers that's nearly as tall as Aaron.

Standing next to the arrangement are Jackson's parents. His mother is a walking tribute to aging well. Mrs. Hunter is wearing a floral designer dress with expensive yet understated jewelry. If I age half as well as she did, I will be grateful.

"Mia! It's so good to meet you," she says as she moves in for a hug. She smells so good. I'd ask what her perfume is, but I'm sure it's not within my budget. She introduces me to her husband. Mr. Hunter's tall and just as handsome as his sons.

"So, you're the reason my son has been walking around smiling like crazy, huh?" I'm not sure what to say, but I can feel my cheeks grow warm. "Jackson, you did alright. It's nice to meet you, Mia," Mr. Hunter says as he embraces me.

"This is my son, Aaron," I reply once we fall apart.

"Hi," Aaron says with a toothy grin.

"Well, you're just too adorable for words. Come here, let me look at you," she says, taking him in.

"Hey, my turn," Mr. Hunter says. He turns his attention to Aaron, who is trying to sneak a peek at the food being placed in the dining hall across from us. Mr. Hunter's voice is booming and serious as he speaks to Aaron.

"Now, I don't care for slackers. So, you have a job?"

Aaron looks up at me, not sure what to say, and I hold back my laughter.

"Well, son, do you?"

"Ah, no…" Aaron says.

"You married?"

He giggles. "No."

"No job and no wife, what do you do then?"

Aaron shrugs his shoulders and grips my hand. "I um…go to school."

"Oh, well, that's more like it. You work hard in school?"

"Yeah," Aaron says with newfound confidence.

"Well, if that's the case, then I guess you can stay and have dinner with us. A hardworking young man needs to be fed. Dinner's not quite ready yet. I know I saw some young people who looked to be about your age—they said they were my grandchildren, so I had to let them in the house. They are around here somewhere…now, where were they going…oh yes, to the game room."

"Game room?!" Aaron replies as his eyes light up.

"Yes, it's an arcade room with toys and other such craziness. You wouldn't be interested in seeing it, would you?" If Aaron nods any harder, his head will snap right off.

"Well, now, you have to ask your mom if you can go," Mr. Hunter says. Aaron looks at me as if his very life depends on my next thought.

"Go ahead, honey," I reply.

"Come on; I'll show you the way," Mr. Hunter says. Aaron takes off like a rocket.

"Don't run!" I yell after him. It's too late; he's already gone. Mrs. Hunter laughs.

"There's nothing he can break in this house that my boys and my grandkids haven't already broken. Don't you worry about it. Come on in here," she says as she walks me towards the dining hall.

"You all go ahead; I need to speak to Mia, alone," his mother says. I exchange a worried glance with Jackson. He smiles reassuringly and kisses my cheek.

"You'll be fine," he says.

I agree to a chat with his mom. She takes me to her charming and fragrant garden in the back and asks me to sit on the bench next to her.

"This is my favorite place in the house. This is where I go when those boys are turning my heart into a yo-yo with their high-speed chases and warehouse raids," she says. She's joking, but only partly. Jackson told me when his mom is anxious because one of them hasn't checked in and is out in the field, she goes to the garden.

"I can't imagine what it's like to worry that much. I worry about Aaron, and he's just one kid. But to worry about five? I don't know how you do it."

"Edibles."

I chuckle, and she looks over at me and raises her eyebrows. Wait, is she serious? "Mrs. Hunter, you don't…"

"Shhh, the boys don't know. It's not all the time. Just every once in a while during book club, and when the boys go on cases that are especially dangerous. I have a guy—Banshee. He gets me what I need. A brownie, a cookie, whatever."

"Wow, okay. I guess if it helps relax you and it's not like you have kids at home, so…What did you want to talk about?"

"I usually run background checks on the women my boys are dating. They don't always listen to me. That's not the way I raised them. They have their own minds. But I look out for them like they would look out for me."

"If you want me and Aaron to go—"

"Certainly not."

"This isn't about what you found out about me?"

"Yes."

"You're going to tell him to leave me?"

"I am going to tell him the same thing I'm telling you. You are now part of this family. Your worries are ours. So whoever or whatever is after you is after us. We will take care of you, and more importantly, Jackson will."

"You're okay with us being together?"

"Without a doubt."

"Why? I thought the background check…"

"I don't need your background check. Someone vouched for you."

"Jackson?"

"Men know nothing. The person who vouched for you is Shelby."

"Shelby stood up for me?"

"Yes, she came into my office and said, 'Her background check is blank. But take her in. Bring her close.' Shelby's protective of this family. If she says you're worth it, you must be."

"Can I ask, what's her story?"

"You know how brave and courageous my boys are?"

"Yeah, I've heard the stories."

"Well, not one of them can measure up to the courage Shelby has shown. And they know that. They have their fun teasing her, but at the end of the day, they'd die for that woman. And she'd gladly die for them."

"Sounds like she's really something," I reply, mostly to myself.

"My sons always pick great women. And I see that Jackson is continuing that tradition. You are raising a sweet kid, and I'm told it's only yourself doing so."

"My ex wasn't cut out for fatherhood."

"It's easy to tell Jackson's taken by you. I just want to know that you feel the same way."

"I do! Jackson is everything I ever wanted in a guy."

"You love him?"

"Yes. Very much."

"Good. Then tell him whatever it is you're hiding. Because while Shelby didn't tell me all there is to know about you, she did mention the discrepancy in your name. And if you want this to work, I'm thinking Jackson should meet Mia Avery."

Chapter 16

Mia

Jackson's mom and I enter the large stylish dining hall. It has high ceilings, French doors, and an antique chandelier. The long dining table in the center of the room has been beautifully set. Three of Jackson's brothers are in attendance, in addition to their wives. They greet me warmly, and I feel bad that I actually hesitated to come inside.

"Are we missing someone?" I ask.

"Shelby and my brother are out of the country. He doesn't get a lot of downtime, so when he has time off, he always whisks Shelby away," Wyatt explains.

"Trust me, when that woman is on vacation, we're all on vacation," Logan quips.

"She's a lovely woman," Jackson's mom says.

"C'mon, Mom, Endless is exhausting," Jackson replies.

"No, she's wonderful, and you need to stop calling her that," Shay scolds Jackson.

"Mia, come have a seat," Skylar says. I go over who's who in my head. Skylar is the first-grade teacher, and she's married to Cash. They have twins. I ask where they are and Skylar says they are upstairs sleeping.

"Speaking of kids, I should probably check on mine," I remark to Jackson. He walks towards the panel on the wall where a white box is mounted. It looks like some kind of security system. He taps on a few keys, and the monitor display turns on. I am watching Aaron play with Jackson's niece and nephews in the game room. He's having the time of his life.

"Don't worry, Mia; we'll call them down when everything is ready," Winter promises.

Jackson walks me to the table, and we sit side by side. The staff enters and begins placing large stainless-steel chafing dishes on top of the tables along the walls. The buffet they are setting up smells heavenly. My mouth waters and I remind myself that it would be wrong to open up the lids and start tasting everything. But then I spot someone doing just that.

"Logan! We haven't started dinner yet," his mother scolds.

"C'mon, old lady; you know we don't stand on ceremony here, I'm starving," Logan replies as he takes a chunk out of an herb-roasted turkey leg. Logan is a little taller than Jackson and just as sexy. "You don't want your only son to starve, do you?" Logan asks.

"Hey, you're not her only son!" Wyatt reminds him.

"That's right, I have four lovely sons," Mrs. Hunter replies.

"Four?" Jackson asks.

"Well yes, I used to have five, but I've demoted you."

Wyatt and Cash start laughing. "What have I been demoted to?" Jackson asks, pretending to be wounded.

His mom thinks for a moment and then says, "Distant cousin, twice removed. The kind that we forget to invite over to Thanksgiving dinner. You know, the kind of relative whose name you misspell in the Christmas card."

I didn't mean to laugh, but I did, and Jackson's mouth dropped. "Really, babe, you're taking her side?"

"Well…a month is a long time not to call your mom," I reply.

"Hey, I am not the worst son in here. Logan convinced Rose to get inside a box so he could ship her to Florida," Jackson says pointedly.

"She wanted to go to Disney World; I was doing her a favor," Logan explains.

"You put her in a box?" I ask.

"I made an air hole," Logan says. I shake my head in disbelief.

His mom continues the story. "I was downstairs, and I saw Logan stumping down the steps with a big cardboard box. He said he was throwing out old toys. Then I heard Rose cough."

"Rose was worse because when Mom saw her, the first thing she said was, 'Cash made me do it,'" Logan says.

"I wasn't even home at the time. You see, Mia, you see how I get blamed for things that I didn't do. The fact is, I was and continue to be the perfect son," Cash adds.

"Lies! All lies! I was the perfect son," Wyatt informs me.

Logan replies, "That's because you were too scared of Mom to get in trouble. But me, I'd get in trouble even when I didn't do anything wrong. My sweet mother grounded me for driving to the store to get chips."

"You were twelve!" his mother reminds him.

"Yeah, but I wore my seatbelt the whole time."

"You did what? God, you guys were awful," I reply.

"Okay, we had issues, but don't let Mom fool you. She had her moments too," Jackson says.

"Me? You would pick on a fragile old woman with fading eyesight?" Mrs. Hunter says, adding a well-placed cough at the end of her speech. The women and I laugh as she winks at us surreptitiously.

"Don't even try it, old lady. Mia, my first day being a cop, in fact, my very first hour on the force, our mother decided to tail me," Wyatt says.

"You followed him?" I ask her.

"Well yes, just to make sure he didn't encounter anything he couldn't handle. And I was very helpful, wasn't I?" she asks Wyatt.

"The guy I arrested was smoking weed and spraying graffiti on the wall. I go up to him. I feel very professional, like yeah, I got this handled. And then my mother gets out of her car, grabs my suspect by the ear, and forces him to apologize for his actions. Then she makes him call his mother and tell her what he's done."

"Are you serious? What happened to the guy?" I ask.

"Oh, he grew up to be a fine young man. He still writes," she says. Wyatt rolls his eyes.

"My point is my mom gave as good as she got. When I came home drunk for the first time in my life, she removed every piece of furniture from my room," Jackson adds.

"That's right. I told you to stay away from drinking. Beds are for boys who listen," she playfully scolds. She turns her attention over to me. "And Mia, I meant to tell you this earlier; you really should be careful about consorting with strangers," she pointedly says as she looks at Jackson.

"Sorry, Mrs. Hunter, he just followed me inside," I joke. Jackson groans and rolls his eyes at me.

"He does look a little like my son Jackson. But he'd never show his face after writing me out of his life."

"I didn't write you out; I was busy," Jackson says, bemused.

"Oh, well I understand that," his mother replies. "I was busy once too—giving birth to you. Sacrificing my waistline." Jackson groans louder. His mom turns to me and whispers just loud enough for him to hear, "I hope one day Aaron doesn't discard you like one of my former sons…now, what was his name, Jason? Johnson? Joe?" Jackson laughs and goes over to her. He places his arms around her neck and pleads for her forgiveness.

"Perhaps," she teases.

"Alright, woman, what do you want to get me off your hit list?" Jackson says.

"I get whatever I want?" she asks.

"Yes, whatever you want," he says. The brothers are already shaking their heads, knowing that their mom is up to something.

"Bachelor. Auction."

The brothers burst out laughing. The women explain that their mom has an auction for charity every year and that the brothers hate it because the women are feisty old ladies who have no shame or issue with grabbing and tearing the bachelors' clothes off. In fact, the brothers would rather face armed gunmen than the crowd of old ladies at the auction.

"No; not gonna happen," Jackson says.

"Okay…" his mom says simply. And although she doesn't speak, her silence is loud.

"I can't do it, Mom. I have a girl now, and she'd be really offended, right baby?" Jackson says.

"What's the charity?" I ask.

"Really?" Jackson mutters under his breath.

"Wounded Warriors" she says.

I look over at Jackson. "Honey, it's for wounded vets…"

"Okay, you and I are on a break, Mia. Seriously. I don't think it's gonna work," Jackson jokes.

His brothers laugh at him. Then from the corner of my eye, I see Winter and Shay whispering to each other. I know something's up.

Then Shay nonchalantly says, "You know what would make the auction really successful this year? A swimsuit portion."

"NOOOOOOOO!" Jackson begs. We all laugh as he buries his head on my chest in sheer agony.

Soon the staff has everything all set up; we thank them and call the kids to come eat. Aaron and the other boys are in the middle of a friendly, but serious debate about who is the strongest X-Man. Add to that the fact that he has shark-shaped grilled cheese on his plate, and my son is in heaven.

I can't believe I was worried about these people. They are so nice and easygoing. I feel as if I've been a part of their family for years. Jackson places his hand on mine under the table and then whispers, "You okay, baby?"

I look into his eyes and reply, "No, I'm more than okay. I'm happy."

One of the staff members enters the room and hands Mrs. Hunter a small long box.

"Mom, what is that?" Wyatt asks.

"Oh, it's not for me; it's for Mia. I'm guessing Jackson got her something."

I look over at Jackson. "Did you?" I ask as I open the box.

Jackson shrugs and says, "No. I didn't get you anything."

"Liar," I tease as I open the box.

It's a black rose.

The color drains from my face. I'm shivering, and I can't think. I can't think. I hear Jackson off in the distance asking what's wrong. I can't reply. I don't remember how to talk.

Is he out there? Is he looking for me? Is he already inside? Should I take Aaron and run? Is it too late?

"Mia, what is it? What's wrong, baby?" Jackson begs. The entire mood of the table has shifted. Everyone is concerned and on high alert. My cell rings. I don't want to pick it up, but I have to know; I have to know if it's really him on the other end.

"Hello?" I say into the phone in a weak whisper.

"You made me do this. Don't forget that," Gorman says; then, without any further warning, a loud, earsplitting "pop" sound shakes the whole house. Something explodes into a fireball, just outside.

The room that once held lighthearted, carefree guys now holds a room full of armed, vigilant, pissed-off cops. All five of them are suddenly armed, including their dad. And all of them are ready.

They push the women and children out of the way and order us to take cover. All five of them go outside. Jackson orders his mom to take the kids to the panic room. Mrs. Hunter does as instructed. Aaron calls out to me, and I tell him it's okay, go with Mrs. Hunter. Jackson is the first to come back; his face is dark with anger. He addresses me not as my boyfriend, but as a no-nonsense special agent in the FBI.

"Someone just blew up your car. Mia, what the fuck is going on?"

Chapter 17

Jackson

Now that we have looked around the area and confirmed whoever did this is gone, and everyone is safe, my focus changes. It's all on Mia. I make my way toward her, but Logan comes between us. He knows just how pissed and enraged I am because he's been there. So, he makes sure to position his body between us so that I would have to go through him to talk to Mia. He speaks to me in a low, deep voice that makes him sound more like the SWAT leader he is rather than my brother.

"Hey, not now. You have questions. I get that. But not here. And not now," he commands.

I look over his shoulder and into Mia's frightened eyes. Logan's right. This is not the time. I try to handle this like a routine case. It helps me to focus on procedure and method. The house floods with different branches of law enforcement and emergency personnel. Wyatt and I handle them while my other brothers try to keep all the kids calm.

Aaron is calling out for his mom and me. Mia and I exchange a look and tend to Aaron. At first, he's scared because he has no idea what happened, but we explain that it was an accident and that no one was hurt. Soon, Aaron and the other kids are asking their parents if they can go see the burned car and take pictures because it's cool. They go over the story, and each time, add their own drastic take on it. I have a feeling this story will be making the rounds at school. Once we are all satisfied that Aaron and the other kids are okay, I go over to Mia.

"Outside, now."

We walk out the door and onto the street. But I don't want to talk anywhere near the house and chance Aaron overhearing us, or anyone else for that matter. We walk about a block down in silence. When I finally stop walking and confront her, my anger hasn't diminished at all.

"Mia, what is going on—and please try really hard not to lie to me this time."

"I have a stalker; his name is Gorman. He's after me. He has been for a long time."

"ARGH! How could you do this? How could you keep this from me?" I demand.

"I was going to tell you."

"When were you going to tell me? Before or after Argo and I had to ID your corpse?" I reply as my heart pounds inside my chest. I can feel her anxiety from where I stand. But I don't care; she fucking needs to hear this.

"I asked you straight out if someone was after you, and you lied to me!" I bark.

"I had to."

"No, you didn't *have* to. You chose to."

"Jackson, I needed to keep you out of this."

I laugh bitterly and look up at the sky. "Oh my God, you don't get it, do you? I am already in this. We're together, Mia. Someone has been after you for only God knows how long, and instead of allowing me to protect you, you lie to me. You keep me in the dark. That makes no sense."

"I wanted to handle things myself. You don't deserve to be pulled into this."

"No, what I don't deserve is to be lied to by the woman I love. I have done everything I can to make you a part of my life, and then you do this?" I rake my hands through my hair so hard I damn near rip the roots out. The rage that's flowing through me is unlike anything I've experienced. She takes a step towards me, and I back away from her.

"Jackson, I know it was wrong to wait so long to tell you, but I—"

"You didn't tell me, so stop making it sound like you told me something later than you should have. The fact is you didn't tell me anything. I had no idea what was going on. We talked day in and day out. And you never said a word. Do you have any idea what could have happened?"

"I know how bad this could have been. I do. Look, it's not always easy to open up to someone."

"Oh really, Doc? It's not easy? Because you have made a career out of getting people to talk to you. But now that it was your turn to be open you bailed."

"I know..."

"What made you think it was okay to keep this from me?" I bark.

"I was trying to protect you from this situation."

"You didn't think I could handle one guy? Are you kidding me?"

"It's not about that. You don't know Gorman; he's not right in the head. I had to do drastic things to get out from under him. I even changed my name and—"

"Wait, your name? You're not Mia Samuels?" I ask, beside myself.

"No."

I laugh sardonically, place my hands on the back of my neck, and let the weight of my stress pull my head down. What the fuck is happening right now? I feel like a fucking idiot.

"Look, I'm sorry, but I had to protect Aaron and—"

"No, don't do that! Don't bring Aaron into this. This is about you and me. You kept me out of this because you still think you have to be a one-woman army. You don't trust that I will have your back. You think I will bail on you like Tom."

"That's not true! Jackson, I should have opened up to you, but it's just not easy to let someone in."

"And that's what I am to you, just 'someone'?"

"No; that's not what I meant."

"I poured my heart out to you. I told you how much of my soul death has taken. I told you about Rose, and Green, and how fucking awful it is to lose the people that I love. And you sat there in mortal danger the whole time, and didn't say shit to me."

"It was my problem, not yours. And I wanted to fix it."

"I HAD A RIGHT TO KNOW!" I yell. She jumps when my voice booms and fills the street.

"Jackson, forgive me."

"You and Aaron could have died tonight. You and that little boy are my whole fucking world, and that could have been taken away tonight. All because you wouldn't come to me. How do I forgive that?" I shake my head angrily and start to walk off.

She reaches out and latches both hands onto my forearm. "Jackson, don't go. Let's talk. We love each other."

I shake my head in disbelief and pull away. "Love? Mia, I don't even know your name…"

I didn't plan to walk for as long as I did. But I was so lost in thought that I walked for about two miles. I end up at my dad's favorite donut shop. I walk in and order a cup of black coffee. It's a good thing they don't serve alcohol. I'm not sure how far down that rabbit hole I would go tonight.

When my dad walks in, I can't say I'm all that surprised to see him. He comes here often after he lies to my mom about where he's headed. She knows he's lying, and I overheard her say once, "Men can't keep secrets from women. But a nice woman will play along so he believes he has some."

Dad takes a seat at the counter next to me and orders us two donuts each and more coffee.

"I'll have two glazed, and my son here, he'll have the chocolate cream," Dad tells the owner. The man takes the donuts down from the tray and places them on plates in front of us.

"I'm not hungry, Dad. And even if I was, I don't like chocolate cream."

"Well, I'm your father, and I love you. If that means I have to help you finish off two donuts, then I will be strong and do my part." I smile despite myself. It's a small smile, one that fades quickly.

"Are they okay?" I ask.

"Aaron and the other boys were still excited about seeing the ball of fire. They are in the game room reenacting what they would have done if they were caught in that situation if it were a movie and they were the heroes. The 'heroes' ate a dozen hot dogs, and when I left, they were finishing off a bag of chips. Your mother made us bring them sleeping bags, so now it's officially a sleepover."

"I'm glad he's okay. He's a good kid," I reply as I take a sip of my black coffee.

"And what about her? You didn't ask if she's okay," Dad says as he takes a bite of his donut. I fake indifference, shrug my shoulders, and look away. He laughs at me.

"What's so funny?" I ask.

"It's all you can do to stay in that chair; you love her so much. You can't hide that from me."

"Yeah, well…is she okay?" I ask again.

"Yes, son, she's okay. But she's scared of this guy and what he might do. And she's worried that you won't ever forgive her."

"She should have talked to me."

"She's stubborn. You were the same way when you were a kid—stubborn to the damn bone."

"That's not the way I remember it."

"The hell you don't. Remember when you and Logan kept running up and down the staircase chasing each other? I said if you two don't stop, there won't be any camping for the rest of the summer. You two didn't listen. Logan ran up the staircase, and you ran after him, fell, and dislocated your shoulder.

"I swear to God I could hear that thing pop out of place. I ran over to you, sure that you'd be crying bloody murder. But no, you tried to keep a straight face, all because you wanted to go camping. I told you, 'Son, you're hurt. You need a doctor.' And what did you do?" he asks.

"I asked what time we were heading out to the camping trip," I reply.

"And while you were doing that, tears were running down your face. You were in so much damn pain, but you wanted to pretend like it didn't hurt. You and that woman you love are the same. Both of you think that there's strength in standing alone and pretending you are okay. But you got it wrong. Strong people admit when they hurt."

"Why didn't she come to me? I would have helped her."

"Like you're helping her right now?" he pointedly says.

I lower my head, and he pats my back and speaks earnestly. "Jackson, she fell. She's hurt. She needs you. Get over your anger; get over your pride. The woman you love is in danger, the kind of danger that could take her away from you forever. So suck that shit up and be the man I raised you to be."

He's right. He knows that. He polishes off his donuts and "helps" me with mine. I place a few bucks on the counter and thank him for his advice.

"Advice? I'm your damn father; this isn't advice," he says in a gruff voice. "It's an order. Go fix this. Now."

"Okay, Dad, I'm on it."

Just as I head out the door he says, "Hey, son, let's not tell your mom about this little talk taking place at a donut shop. We met up at the bar down the street."

"Where you had a sensible salad?"

"With a light dressing."

I laugh. "You got it, Dad. And thanks."

"And Jackson, you make things right with my future daughter-in-law. You hear me?"

"Yeah, Dad, I hear you."

I take my dad's car back, that way he has to walk off the donuts and I won't feel bad about having to lie to Mom about what he ate. When I pull up to the front of the house, things are very still and quiet. All the cop cars and law enforcement are gone. She's standing on the front porch with her arms folded across her chest. I can see the worry in her eyes from here. My chest tightens as I gaze on her small frame. I can't believe how much I love this woman.

"Hey," I whisper as I come up to her.

"Mia Avery. That's my name. I'm sorry. I'm so sorry," she says as tears spill down her face.

"I know, baby," I reply as I hold her in my arms. "We'll figure this out," I promise her.

She pulls away. "You sure you want to be involved? I mean, you want to know the whole story?"

"You're my family. And so is Aaron. It's my story too now."

"Okay, I…I'm not sure where to start."

"Well, let's start with a change of venue. Someone told me that could help," I reply, referencing her advice to me when I was trying to come clean about the raid.

"You want to go somewhere? I guess we can. Aaron and the others fell asleep a little while ago," she says.

"Let's go to my house."

"Is Aaron gonna be okay here? I mean if he wakes up…"

"He's safe here. You know that, don't you?"

"Yeah, I do."

"We'll pick him up first thing in the morning. We really need to talk—alone."

"You're right. I'm gonna check in with your mom and officially ask her, and then look in on Aaron. Be right back," she says as she runs back inside. Soon we are in my car and headed home for the most overdue conversation in the world.

Chapter 18

Jackson

When we get to my place, I make her some tea, and we settle in. The woman sitting on the sofa isn't the Mia I know. I have never seen that much fear in her eyes. That woman, who laughed often and moved about the world with ease, has retreated into a shy, uncertain creature. Even before she tells me her story, I am pissed off by whoever has made my woman so damn fearful. And just before she begins, I have to remind my anger to take a back seat to her needs.

"Baby, you can take your time with me. You know that. I'm here, and I'm not going anywhere," I promise. She brings her knees up to her chest and wraps her arms around herself. She looks so small; my chest tightens, and I try to prepare for what she's about to say.

"It started three years ago. I was living in Hartford, Connecticut. It was just after Tom and I split. I had just bought my first house. I had worked my ass off to make it happen. It was a small starter home, but it meant the world to me. It was the first step in Aaron and me starting our new lives.

"It was hard because I had to come to terms with the fact that Tom and I were officially over, in addition to the fact that I was now a single parent. But eventually, things got easier, and we started to adjust to our new situation.

"One day, Aaron got sick—strep throat. We went to the doctor and got the antibiotics he needed. I didn't have the heart to leave him with a sitter, so I worked from home. Later that day, my Internet went down. I called the company, and they sent someone over to fix the problem. His name was Mark Gorman. He was a lanky, unassuming, middle-aged guy with glasses—the kind of guy that people tend to overlook.

"It was nearly a hundred degrees the day I first met Gorman. He was sweating, and his face was red. I offered him a bottle of ice water, and he took it. He remarked that none of his other customers had ever done that, and thanked me. I said, 'anytime.' And then I showed him to my office.

"I went to check on Aaron; he was sound asleep. Then I took a call from a girlfriend of mine. We talked about our misguided attempts to 'find ourselves' back in high school. I had a phase where I wanted to be a Goth girl. I remarked that while seeing those pictures made me shudder, I still had a thing for black roses. We talked for another ten minutes or so, and then I hung up and went to check on Gorman's progress.

"He said he was almost done. Aaron woke up and heard a male voice and came running into my office. 'Dad?!' he said, still half asleep.

"'No, sweetie, it's not your dad. This is Mark Gorman. He's going to fix Mom's computer.' Aaron waved hello and then went back to bed. Gorman asked where Aaron's dad was, and I didn't say anything. He guessed by my expression that things were over between us. It was kind of awkward, so I said that I would leave him alone so he could finish his work in peace. When he was done, he thanked me for the water again and waved good-bye.

"A week later, the black roses started to appear. I found one on my doorstep. It was followed by a call. The person on the other end didn't say anything. I dismissed it and went on with my day. But soon more roses would appear: on my car window, at my office downtown, and as always, at my front door. The calls increased as well. They were coming in at all hours now. The person never spoke, just breathed into the phone. It was off-putting and frustrating, but I tried to dismiss it as just some stupid prank.

"Then the emails started. It was from an anonymous account. The person wrote that I was their soul mate and that we were meant to be together. I deleted it and blocked that email account. But the person created a new account and sent more emails. It got to the point where I was receiving up to a hundred and sixty emails a day, all from the same person, professing their love to me.

"They demanded that I reply, and even though I knew better, I wrote back. It was a stupid thing to do because stalkers thrive off interaction with their victims. But I couldn't face the fact that I had a stalker. And I certainly did not want to be seen as a victim. So I made myself think this was just a person who was misguided. So I wrote back that I wasn't interested and that I did not want any further contact.

"It worked. Things went back to normal—for a while. But two weeks later, the calls started again. And now he was texting me. I fought changing my number because I didn't want to let this asshole change my life. But soon, I had no choice. He would text me these obscene things that he wanted to do to me. He'd send me disgusting pictures, and I started to feel dread any time my phone rang. So, I gave in and changed my cell number. I also closed my Facebook account because he began to message me there as well.

"I thought that would help things, but it only made it worse. His not being able to contact me sent him into a tailspin. He showed up at my job one evening, demanding to know why I had cut off contact. It took a while to place him as the repair guy. He was so angry; I thought he was going to attack me.

"He motioned towards me, and I flinched. Gorman said, 'Mia, I would never hurt you. You're my life. My love. My only soul mate. That's why you have to behave. You have to be good to me because we're going to be a family. You. Me. And Aaron.'

"Hearing him say my son's name made my blood run cold. I screamed at him to get away from me. I quickly got into my car and took off. I went to the cops, but they said there was nothing they could do unless he actually laid hands on me.

"It turns out changing my cell number was pointless because he found my new number. I didn't know it at the time, but it turns out he had placed a virus on my computer. He had access to my cell records and other bills. He also had a webcam and could turn it on at will from wherever he was.

"Argo and I talked almost every night, and he begged me to move to New York City. He said he'd help me find a place, and that we could start fresh. But I held out. I had just bought the house, and the market was bad. And I didn't want us to leave our home. Also, somewhere deep inside, I still believed that I could handle things.

"Gorman began to follow me around. He kept enough distance to make the cops think I was crazy. He never came to my door, but he'd stand across the street with a black hoodie on and just watch the house. He'd stay there for hours just watching me. After weeks of this, I was finally able to get a restraining order. That gave me some peace of mind for a while. I even allowed myself to think it was over. I went to dinner with a guy friend of mine, Cory, and actually had a nice time.

"When I got back home, I paid the sitter and put Aaron to bed. An hour later, Gorman was pounding on my door. He was calling me a whore and said that he would kill me for betraying him. Aaron was terrified and came to my room crying. I called the cops and held him in my arms. I promised him that everything was going to be okay, but knew I was lying. Nothing was ever going to be okay anymore, not with this lunatic coming after me. He ran away before the cops could get him. And when they went over to his place, he was gone.

"A few days later, the guy I went to dinner with, Cory, was attacked in the parking lot. I know it was Gorman. He disguised himself with shades and a hoodie. He walked up to Cory screaming, 'She's mine. Not yours. Mine!' and then attacked him with a bat. Gorman put Cory in a coma for six weeks.

"And Gorman said it was my fault, that I had broken the rules and hooked up with another guy. He said I soiled our love, and he would make me pay. Things had gotten so out of hand; Tom offered to take Aaron. But I knew Tom couldn't handle Aaron full time. And I didn't want to be separated from my son. But I didn't know what to do.

"Gorman was playing the system. He knew exactly how far he could go to stay within the limits of the law. And even when he did break the law, he'd come to court pretending to be crazy. They would find him guilty, but not competent to stand trial. They'd send him to a psych ward. He'd take his meds for a few weeks, and then when they let him out, he'd be right back to it. He started having mail delivered to my house—pictures of me at home, pictures of me in the parking lot at work. He wanted me to know that no place was safe.

"It got to the point where even when he wasn't following me, I still *felt* him. He got in my head. I became a nervous wreck. I wasn't eating, I could barely sleep, and my hair began to fall out. I couldn't pay attention at work; I had to take a leave of absence. It got so bad, the only place I felt safe was in the closet. I would stay there for hours. Aaron was so scared; I had to send him to his grandmother—Tom's mom. Argo kept begging me to move, but I had worked so hard to start a new life after Tom.

"I wondered what I said, what I did to make this madman think that we were in love. I knew that it wasn't me. I knew that he was mentally unstable and that it didn't require anything on my end for him to become obsessed with me. But knowing it on a professional level didn't ease my mind.

"I started blaming myself. Why did I let him into my house? Why did I give him the water? Did I smile the wrong way? Did I lead him on?"

"That's bullshit; this had nothing to do with you! You did nothing wrong," I plead as I take her hand in mine.

"I knew that in my head, but it didn't stop me from blaming myself."

"Mia…" I can't find the words. I can't begin to imagine living in that kind of hell. Her eyes fill with tears, and I swear my fucking heart is going to burst. I wipe her tears and tell her she doesn't have to continue if she doesn't want to, but she insists.

"I want you to know," she says. I slowly nod and watch her go back to the hell of her past.

"I started seeing a therapist to learn how to cope with what was happening. I turned my cell off for a session, and when I turned it back on, Gorman had sent me a video of him pleasuring himself—in my bed."

"Are you fucking kidding me?" I couldn't stop my outburst. I also can't stop my fist from clenching. I swear to God I'm gonna kill this asshole.

"I called the cops. When they got there, he was gone, and all he left behind was a black rose. I didn't even stop to think. I packed my stuff and headed straight for Argo's apartment. I sold the house. I took a major loss on it, but I didn't care. I changed my last name from Avery to my mom's stepfather's name—Samuels. I cut off most of my ties and didn't tell anyone where I had gone. I wanted to be free from Gorman. I wanted my life back. But now I know I will never be free," she sobs. I take her in my arms and hold her firmly.

"There's no fucking way Gorman is getting to you or Aaron. You hear me? There's no way. I'll cut him in half before he gets anywhere near you."

"I don't care about me, Jackson; I can't uproot Aaron again. He's just started making friends; he's happy here. But if we stay and something happens to him…"

I pull her away from my chest so I can look into her eyes.

"Mia, listen to me. I will die before I let anything happen to you and Aaron. I swear on Rose's grave, I will keep you and Aaron safe."

Mia

Jackson asked a lot of questions. It's easy to see how concerned he is and how upset this makes him. He asks how Aaron has been

dealing with things. I tell him that I took Aaron to see a friend of mine who specializes in kids with traumatic experiences. It took some time, but Aaron finally started to feel safe.

Right now, the thing that's making me feel safe is Jackson's powerful, protective embrace. I don't know how long it took for me to stop sobbing. Once I started, I found that I couldn't stop. He didn't judge my actions or my complete breakdown. He just held me and let me openly weep until I was finally all cried out.

At some point in the evening, I exchange my clothes for one of his roomy T-shirts. We end up spooning on the sofa as he holds me firmly against him. The events of the last few days and the memory of all that's happened leaves me drained and exhausted. My eyelids grow heavy, and I give in to sleep.

Tapping on the windowpane wakes me. I open my eyes. There's a light, steady rain falling on the city. The clouds are drained of color and brooding. It's just after six in the morning, and it's hard to believe, but Manhattan is actually still. It's as if all of New York City has been paused so the rain can speak.

I turn to face him. He hasn't slept at all. He's spent the whole night watching over me. His eyes are dark with concern. It's such a heavy story to hand over to someone. I can see it weighs on him. And even though we are lying on the sofa, face-to-face in the most intimate position, he hasn't let his guard down. He's in "protect" mode. He's looking off into the distance, thinking like a cop.

"Where are you?" I softly ask as I look into his face.

He shakes his head in disdain. "I can't believe the things this guy has gotten away with. I can't let that ever happen to you and Aaron again. Gorman can't continue to terrorize you. There's no fucking way," he says in a quiet, steely voice.

"I don't want to think about him. Not right now," I reply as I place my hand against his chest. "Will you do something for me?" I ask.

"Anything," he says, meeting my eyes.

"Make it better. Make this all better…"

He knows what I mean. He knows what I need to be healed right now. He helps me take his shirt off of me. I unbuckle his belt and strip his jeans off. I slide his shirt off him and for a moment, we just stare into each other's eyes. The tenderness he kisses me with rocks me to my core. He nuzzles from my temple down to the nape of my neck. My pulse races as his kisses go from the crux of my elbows down to my wrists.

He brings my hand to his mouth and kisses my palm. He grazes my fingertips along his lips and suckles on my fingers one by one. He causes a warm tingle down my body when he travels to places most men miss—along my collarbone, the curve under my breasts, and the space just above my waist. He brushes his lips along my spine and leaves me shivering. When he strokes the back of my thighs and nuzzles behind my knee, I pant.

He starts kissing along my inner thigh and my eyes flutter with ecstasy. Every inch of me longs for him. My hardened nipples ache for his attention. He doesn't leave them waiting for long. Soon he's suckling and kneading them with his mouth and hands. There are so many sensations going through me; I dig my nails into the skin of his massive biceps to anchor myself.

I want to make him feel as whole and as loved as I do. I flip over so that I'm the one on top; I'm the one with the control. I flick his nipple with my tongue, and he catches his breath. I bathe him with warm, passionate kisses all over. When I reach his inner thigh, his already stiff, large cock stands even more firmly. I tease, kiss, and lick my way towards his member, but I never actually touch it. He groans with anticipation when I make my way towards his cock for the third time. This time, I kiss the head gently over and over until his eyes are glazed with lust and longing.

When I lick the space between his cock and balls, he latches on to me. I slide my tongue down his member and take him inside my mouth; he swears under his breath. The speed, pattern, and rhythm of my tongue sends him so far over the edge that he groans, "Christ baby…"

I move my tongue in unbroken spirals along his cock while I cup and knead his balls. The suction and depth of my mouth causes him to let out an animalistic growl. A growl that damn near shakes the room.

Without warning, he switches position; he's on top. He spreads my legs. His cock grazes my opening. All my nerve endings have been ignited. He doesn't enter me. Instead, he glides his tip against my clit, and it fills me with so much desire, tears spring to my eyes.

He's turned me on so much and made me so wet that I lose touch with reason. I don't wait for him to enter me. I impale myself on his cock. He's a lot to take in. He begins to split me open. My breathing is uneven; my heart is pounding. It hurts. The only thing that would hurt more is if he stopped. I need him. I need all of him.

I demand my body to open up to him, and it does. It opens up in a way it has not done with anyone else. He watches my breasts bounce up and down as he sinks inside me. I gasp and curl my fingers around his shoulders. With every thrust, he's fucking me, loving me…healing me.

I turn around so that I get to be on top. I don't last long. I come so hard my eyes roll to the back of my head. My legs shake, and the wind is ripped from my lungs. I propel forward and fall onto his chest. He wraps his arms around me, and I hold on for dear life as he climaxes. When it's over, we hold on to each other. It's a silent promise we make—no matter what, hold on to each other.

Chapter 19

Mia

In the days following the car explosion, everything changed. Jackson wouldn't let Aaron and me return home. He asked that we move in with him. I suggested a hotel because I didn't want to invade his space. But while I was still thinking it over, Jackson and Aaron were already going shopping for his new room.

The number one thing on their list: fish tank. Aaron has wanted a fish tank for a while now, but our old place didn't allow it. Moving in is ordinarily a huge chore, but with the Hunter brothers and their wives, we were settled in no time. I mentioned something about not having enough time to fix everything once we got in the house, and the next thing I knew, I got a visit from Shelby.

She cut her vacation short to come help out. She made a few well-placed calls, and within a few days, the townhouse was decorated and felt like home. On one of our shopping days, Shelby arranged to meet at my office. That's when she first encountered Argo. They hit it off right away.

"Oh honey, those shoes are giving me life!" Argo said to Shelby once he spotted her red heels.

"Well, that makes sense; half of New York City has been *dying* to get them."

The two of them laughed, and ever since then, they've had a "fashion" shortcut. He looks her outfit over as soon as she walks into the office.

"Bag?" he says.

"Prada."

"Shoes?"

"Christian."

"Dress?"

"Stella."

"Yes!"

"Yes!"

When the three of us are together, we laugh a lot more than I ever thought we would. I wasn't going to decorate at all at first, but then Jackson suggested it. I reminded him we were only staying until they found Gorman and he said, "You came here because of him, but I want you to stay because of us." And so Aaron and I are here to stay.

The most significant part in all of this is that for the first time, I don't feel alone. All the brothers are working to track Gorman down. They've found out what institution he was in for the past few years, and where he stayed when he first got into the city. They are seriously doing everything they can, including taking turns playing bodyguard. I told them it wasn't necessary, and they said they were under orders from Jackson.

I kept thanking Jackson for helping me, and he pointed out that being with me has helped him too. I said sex doesn't count. He laughed and said he was referring to having fixed things with Megan.

"How'd you make that happen?" I asked one night after dinner.

"I thought about what you said, about focusing on the good parts of Green's life. Like how happy he was after he passed his firearms exam. So, I thought it would be good to show her that side of it.

"We record exams at the agency, and I got permission to show her his recording. She got to see how excited he was, and how much he loved finally being able to work in the field. It didn't make everything better, but I think it gave her some peace," he said.

He was right about that. A few days later, Megan went into labor and sent us a picture of her new baby girl. I think that helped both Megan and Jackson move on.

I wish we didn't have Gorman to worry about because my new life with Jackson would be perfect. I make dinner for him and Aaron; he tries to make it home in time, and more often than not, he does. We sit at the table, talk, joke around, and catch up on each other's day. I can't remember a time when I wasn't with Jackson, and that's how I know he's the man I've been looking for all this time.

I'd like to say that all the good stuff in my life outweighs Gorman, but it doesn't. I find myself looking over my shoulder and always on edge. I will have good moments, like dinnertime, but for a vast portion of the day, I worry.

I think Jackson knows that and that's why he's trying to distract me by asking me to go to a party. I said no at first, but then his mom called and said it was a benefit for the "Feed America" program. It's an organization that provides food to homeless families. How could I turn that down? She asked for my help to sweet-talk some of the wealthy donors into giving more money.

And now, we are in the middle of Mrs. Hunter's home, and the benefit is in full swing. I want to work hard and get them as many donations as I can, so I work the room and hope for the best. I notice a certain hot FBI agent checking me out from across the room. I am a lucky girl.

Jackson

That woman across the room is going to be my wife. I asked Aaron's blessing first, and he gave it to me. So, I got her ring last night. Thanks to Argo's expert eye, we found a ring that's perfect for her: vintage and classy. I can't process the kind of happiness I've been feeling. I know she'll say she doesn't need a big ceremony, but Shelby and Argo have other plans. Our wedding will be elegant and gorgeous whether we like it or not. That's one thing I can say for Endless, that woman can plan a party.

I hear Mia laugh a few yards away from me. I'm so glad my mom talked her into coming tonight. She's been so stressed lately. I understand; I'm feeling it too. I need this guy contained as soon as possible. My drive to find Gorman increases with every passing day. How dare he fuck with my family? How dare he terrify a little kid? It doesn't matter, as Gorman won't be a problem for long—I guarantee it.

I hear her laugh again. God, I love that laugh. I watch her work the room with ease and grace. Anyone she's speaking to gets her undivided attention, and it makes them feel special. She maintains eye contact and keeps them engaged. Her genuine, intoxicating laugh draws people over to her. Once they are near her, they can't help but be pulled in by her warmth, humor, and intellect. It's easy to see she's in her element.

She has turned more than a few heads. In fact, there are at least four men so far who are having trouble looking away from her. They gaze at her lethal curves, pouty lips, and supple breasts. They look at her like she just stepped out of their wet dream and into real life. I swallow my initial wave of jealousy, but soon, all I want is to take her away and have her all to myself.

I walk towards her and whisper in her ear. "Every guy here is eye fucking you. It's making me crazy," I admit, knowing I sound like a fool.

"What guys? All I see is you," she says as she gazes into my eyes. Before I can reply, she walks away and goes to entertain a group across the room from us. But from that moment on, every action she takes is to get my attention.

During the evening, she comes by where I am seated and reaches over me to get a glass, allowing me a perfect view of her firm ass. Later on, she sees me at the bar but doesn't address me. Instead, she sits across the bar and casually dips a large chocolate covered strawberry into her champagne glass. She coils her tongue around the fruit and gingerly licks it. The room starts to grow quiet as I watch her dip and lick the strawberry. My pulse races as she wraps her mouth around the supple flesh of the fruit and bites down. The juice oozes out from the fruit and dribbles down her lips.

Damn her.

She makes sure I see her leave the bar. I follow her down the hallway, where she enters the library. I follow her, but she slips out of the back door. Seconds later, she texts me:

"Graze on my lips; and if those hills be dry,
Stray lower, where the pleasant fountains lie."

Argh! Damn this woman. She's turning me on and frustrating me at the same time. But I know that no matter what, I need to find where that damn quote is from. I look it up on my cell—it's one of Shakespeare's plays, *Venus and Adonis.* I quickly scour the library and find the Shakespeare section. I never in my life thought I'd care that much about plays. I look past the more prevalent plays and finally land on the play in question. I open the book and find the treasure she left for me—it's soft, lacy, and powder blue.

Christ.

My woman is walking around this event sexy as fuck with no damn panties on. I bring the soft material to my face and inhale her heady scent. I have to find her and fuck her. Now.

"Where are you?" I text.

"Hope you enjoyed the preview. Can't wait for us to get home," she texts back.

Home? She's fucking crazy! No way I'm gonna wait. It's taken all my focus to keep from being rock hard. Then she goes and takes off her panties? And now she wants me to wait. No fucking way.

"I'm coming for you," I vow.

"You wouldn't dare, not here," she texts. I don't bother to reply. I seek her out with the same fervor I would if she were a fugitive on the run. I spot her in a crowd that includes my parents and their friends.

"I need to speak with you," I whisper in her ear.

"Maybe later, okay?" she says, pleading with her eyes.

"No, now," I reply with a smile. She started this, and I'm gonna finish it. She looks into my eyes and sees that I'm serious about taking her away. She excuses us, and we make our way down the hallway.

"Okay, Jackson, I know I'm the one who started this but—" Before she can finish, I pull her into the coat closet and close the door behind us. We can hear the crowd of partygoers just outside the door, and there's no lock at all, meaning someone could walk in on us at any time. I. Don't. Care.

I start kissing her with a need that is too strong to be absolutely satisfied. She kisses back, and groans as our tongues dance and collide with each other. I pull my pants down, hoist her up so that her legs are wrapped around my waist, and slam her against the wall.

I yank her dress down, and she slips the straps of her bra down to expose her ripe, hard, pink nipples. I gather a fistful of her hair and yank down on it until her back arches up and her nipples and my mouth align. I suckle on her extended tips until they are swollen and glistening. I fervently trail kisses down her throat while my fingers slip between the slick folds of her pussy.

She's so wet, so ready.

Her hips grind against my fingers, and she moans with longing. She wraps her legs even tighter around me as my fingers control her. Outside, there are footsteps approaching, but we don't stop; we can't. Somewhere along the way, the person takes a turn, and the closet door remains closed—for now. We should stop, but we don't. Her tight pussy is too wet and feels too good.

"Grab my cock, baby. Put me inside you."

The sensation of her delicate fingers wrapped around the base of my shaft sends me into overdrive. I'm so fucking hard; if I'm not careful, I'll hurt her. She slides her hand up and down my cock to get a feel of how big and how long it is. Her eyes widen. It's bigger and longer than she thought. She's excited, but also nervous.

"There's so much of you," she gasps. I smile and then suck on her earlobe. "Will you be gentle?" she begs.

"No," I reply as I bite down on her earlobe.

"Good," she cries out. She's so focused on the slight pain in her ear, she doesn't pick up on the pressure that's pounding its way between her legs until it's too late, and I'm already inside her. She gasps, and her breathing grows choppy and uneven.

"That's it, I'm in, baby. I'm in," I promise her. She moans and moves so that her body can get used to me. But the longer I'm inside her, the more I lose my mind. "Mia baby, I gotta move, I gotta get in."

"More? You're already so deep."

"No, baby, that's not deep. This is…" I pry her legs further apart and plow into her with an unrelenting force that's bigger than the both of us. She falls forward, using my chest to muffle her erotic cries. She lets my cock make its way to the deepest, softest, most vulnerable parts of her. Sometimes my thrusts are demanding, and sometimes they are giving. But no matter how hard or how deep I penetrate her, she takes me in. Her walls milk me with a reckless abandon unlike anything I've ever encountered.

We are on the brink, and we dare not stop or even slow down. We slam into each other like the tide hitting the shore during a storm. We hear footsteps coming straight for the closet door. They get closer and closer, and unlike before they are not fading away. Someone is about to open the door and see us. I start to slow down, not sure if it's worth the risk, fearing her being exposed.

"Don't you fucking stop," she demands as she uses the walls of her pussy to trap my cock inside her. She rides me with renewed energy; her hips twist in ways that haven't been invented yet. She takes my body on a ride, leaving planet Earth behind. Shit.

"Fuck, baby, you feel so good right now," I plead as we sweat and fuck our way into oblivion. Someone turns the doorknob. They are about to pull the door open. We should be scared, but the only thing I fear is that she'll stop fucking me. And the only fear that comes from her is the fear that my cock will be taken away. Not a chance. We hold on tightly to each other as we ride our way into an orgasm that defies words. When we finally stop jerking and shivering, she collapses onto me. We exchange a long, lingering, gentle kiss.

"Are you okay, baby?" I ask.

"Yeah, I'm very good," she says, beaming.

"You look so goddamn beautiful," I admit as I study her face.

"Remind me to come to all your mom's parties." She laughs. "What happened to the person outside the door?" she asks.

"Somehow, whoever was going to open the closet was diverted by a voice that ordered them to use the other coatroom," I reply.

"Whoever it was that sent them away, we owe them big."

"Yeah, that's what I'm afraid of," I grumble as I help her put her clothes back on.

"Whose voice was it? Who saved us?" she asks.

I sigh and shake my head. "Shelby."

Chapter 20

Mia

We always manage to be just one step behind Gorman, and I can tell it's starting to get to Jackson. It's gotten to the point where his brothers had to take him aside and try to calm him down. They even suggested that he step down and let one of them take the lead. Jackson refused. The brothers understood but made him promise to pause before he did something reckless.

Well, taking a pause didn't help. Jackson got a lead—a guy who traffics in stolen goods got a visit from Gorman, who was looking to buy a gun. Jackson went to the dealer and told him to give up everything he knew about Gorman. The guy said he had a reputation and that he wouldn't talk. Jackson literally threatened to shoot his balls off. The brothers were standing by, and they soon realized it was not a threat. Jackson was going to shoot this guy's cock clean off. It took two of them—Logan and Wyatt—to get Jackson to back off.

I began to fear that this whole mess would make Jackson lose himself. If Jackson becomes a violent, lawless man, then he's letting Gorman change him. And I will be damned if I let anyone change the man I love.

I was looking for a way to remind him about his kinder side and make sure he got in touch with who he was before this Gorman situation. It took some time, but I finally got an idea. Jackson once

"

told me about how when Rose first got so sick she couldn't leave the hospital. They used to like stargazing, but that was not possible anymore.

So, the two of them would put together a puzzle when he came to see her. It wasn't so much the puzzle, but having an activity to focus on helped them ease into their visit. It soon became their thing. He came into her hospital room once, and she wasn't there. His heart nearly stopped thinking that maybe she had passed away in the middle of the night. It turns out they had taken her away, but just to run some tests.

When he told her about what he first thought when she wasn't there, she promised him that she wouldn't die until the puzzle was done. And true to her word, they finished the puzzle. But he loved his sister so much that the thought of her being gone was just one he couldn't take. So he went out and bought a five-thousand-piece puzzle because somewhere in his mind, he hoped that would push her to stay around longer. She died before they could finish it. He left the puzzle, unfinished, in his home office. He never touches it.

I went into his office this morning, and an idea came to mind. I made some calls to the family, and a few hours later, we were all headed for dinner at Wyatt's house. Just before we knock on the door, I tell Jackson what I have planned for him.

"Tonight, the puzzle you started with Rose will get finished."

"What are you talking about? Baby, I told you, I can't finish the puzzle. I was supposed to do it with Rose."

I wrap my arms around his neck and lean in close. "Your whole family is here because they want to help you. I know you can't finish it *with* Rose, but maybe you can finish it *for* her." I smile. He kisses me and happily agrees. We head inside Wyatt's home. Aaron doesn't wait for us; he just takes off to go play with the other kids upstairs.

Wyatt has made a feast, and four of the five brothers are there—everyone except Shelby's husband. There's a table that's been placed at the center of the room, where the puzzle pieces lie. Right away the brothers start playfully arguing about the best strategy to assemble a puzzle.

"Everyone knows you start with the corners!" Logan says.

"That's why you SWAT guys never get shit done!" Cash counters.

"No, you start with the section that has the easiest to fit pieces," Wyatt adds.

Winter rolls her eyes and starts working on the puzzle. "I see once again the women are going to have to rescue you men from yourselves."

The rest of the group joins her. Jackson looks at me from across the table and mouths the words, "Thank you." And for the rest of the evening, we laugh, eat, drink, and help Rose with her final puzzle.

Towards the end of the night, there's a knock on Wyatt's door. He opens it and grins when he sees who is joining us—Shelby and her husband.

"Mia, this is my husband, Gage."

Gage. Is. Fucking. Gorgeous.

Shit, they need to bottle whatever is in the gene pool and sell it. God knows I'd buy it.

I can tell right away that Gage is not like his brothers. He has a certain understated sophistication. His crisp, high-end black button-down shirt, chiseled jaw, and sculpted body make it hard for me to stop staring. I'm lost in his smoldering eyes. He's got a sexy-silent vibe going on. But it's more than that; Gage has an air of mystery. Shelby is lucky she gets to solve it.

Damn.

"You are still in danger?" he asks.

"Yes, but tonight, we are going to put that aside and try to have fun," I reply.

"How long have you been stalked?" he asks.

"Years."

"Not acceptable."

"I know, but—"

He stops me by holding up his hand. He makes a call. "Get me Cannon," he says into the phone. His tone is absolute and leaves no room for argument. "I sent you a name. Where is the suspect's location? ... Not good enough ... you have an hour. Try not to piss me off. Find him. Now." He hangs up and slightly nods towards me. "It's handled. Tell Jackson to be ready."

Gage Hunter wasn't kidding when he said he had it handled. Less than an hour later, SWAT is kicking down Gorman's door on the Lower East Side. According to Jackson, Gage has access to the CIA and Homeland toys that the FBI doesn't.

I promised Jackson that I would stay put and be safe at home. But sitting here in the house is making me crazy; I want to know what's happening. I want to know for sure that the brothers are okay. Ordinarily, I'd have Aaron as a distraction, but he's on a class trip, and I'm off today, so I'm home alone.

I pace up and down the house, not sure what to do. I want to call Argo, but his dad is in town, and the two of them are going out to lunch to talk about graduation. I'm so glad they are getting closer. But Argo is still nervous, and if I call and tell him that Gorman has been spotted, he's going to want to come here and stay with me. I don't want that. He needs to focus on his relationship with his dad.

My cell rings; it's a new phone, so I don't recognize its ringtone at first. When I look down at the screen—speak of the devil. It's Argo calling on video.

"No, Argo, you are not backing out of lunch. If you go, I'll talk you up to the new hot guy at my gym." I laugh, waiting for the video to come into focus. When the screen clears up, it's not Argo I see.

"Hello, Mia."

It's Gorman. My blood runs cold.

Oh my god.

"Where's Argo?! Did you hurt him! Why do you have his phone?" I yell.

"He's tied up at the moment. But why don't you see for yourself," he says. He shows me Argo, head down and tied up in a chair. Everything is spinning.

"Please, don't hurt him," I beg.

"You and I are long overdue for a talk. Come alone. If you don't, I'll be sending you pieces of your friend in the mail for years."

"If you killed him I swear to God—"

"Whatever I do, Mia, it's on you. You should never have tried to end our love."

"WE WERE NEVER TOGETHER, YOU BASTARD!"

"He's still breathing, Mia. But I can stop that. Do you want that? Do you want me to kill him?" he says as he aims the gun at Argo's head.

"NO! Please. I'm coming to you."

"Alone," he reminds me.

"Yes. I'm coming, alone."

"I have access to your cell; make any calls, and I will know about it. There's a car waiting for you downstairs. Get in."

I don't have time to think or even plan. Gorman won't hang up, and he stays on video, making sure that I do nothing but head straight into the awaiting car. We drive for about twenty minutes before the car makes a sudden stop at an abandoned building in downtown somewhere. Gorman orders me to get out and walk into the gutted building.

I do as I'm told and pass a series of decaying rooms with no doors and shattered glass. I go down a hallway with multiple entrances and exits. At the end of the hall is a broken-down elevator. In the middle of the room, I find Argo tied to a chair. He's awake, thank God. But his mouth is tied as well as his hands. I run toward him, but Gorman stops me cold by placing the gun next to Argo's head.

"I'll come to you, but you have to let him go first," I push, forcing myself not to give in to my panic. Being in the same room with Gorman is enough to make me violently ill with fear. But first I need to get Argo to safety.

"You're not here to make deals."

"Bullshit. You want me, fine. But first, you let him get out of here, safe."

"Okay, I can do that. First, you need to come to me."

"For every step I get closer to you, you get him one step closer to his freedom," I order. I don't know where this defiance in me is coming from, but I'm glad it's here. I take one step, and he takes off Argo's restraints. By the time I'm halfway to him, he has let Argo walk further out. Then I see it in his eyes—a cruel and malicious cloud. He's going to shoot Argo just to spite me.

"Argo, watch out!" I shout.

He takes cover behind one of the pillars. Gorman yanks me to him and places me in a chokehold.

"Not to worry, Mia. I won't let you lose consciousness," he vows. "I want you awake for all of it! All of it!"

I hear footsteps coming from the entrance. Jackson is here. I don't know how. Wait—the new phone. He must have placed a tracker on it.

"Argo, get out of here; call 911," Jackson orders.

"Do not move!" Gorman says.

"Argo, leave. Now," Jackson repeats in a commanding tone.

"I have a gun, what makes you think I won't take him out?"

"Because this isn't about him. It's about you and Mia. So, let's just keep it about that. Argo, get the fuck out of here, now!" Jackson barks. Argo reluctantly runs out of the building.

"How'd you know I was here?" Gorman asks.

"I knew you'd want to be alone with her. She's your weakness, Gorman. I knew that wherever she was, you'd eventually be. So I let everyone else check out your hiding spot. But I stayed with her."

"You stayed behind, saw her get into the car, and followed, clever man you are."

"You have no idea," Jackson says. I know Jackson is looking for a way to get a clean shot, but Gorman is using me as a shield.

"I will put a bullet in her if you don't back up."

He holds the gun at my head with one hand and wraps his arm around my neck with the other. I try in vain to break free from his hold. He walks backwards toward the open elevator shaft and calls out to Jackson.

"Stay away from us, or I'll kill her right here and now," he vows.

"Let her go, Gorman! There's nowhere for you to run. Let her go, and we can talk about this," Jackson says.

"No! This is all her fault! She made me love her. She promised me forever with her eyes and then she betrayed me!" he screeches at the top of his lungs.

He demands that Jackson put his weapon down, and Jackson says he can't do that. My mind is a blur of panic, fear, and adrenaline.

"Did she tell you that she came on to me?" Gorman says as he begins to cry. "She told me she loved me. She said it with her body. That first day I met her, I knew she was mine. I had to have her. But things got so bad. She took to me court; she tried to have me locked up. She's been bad. Haven't you, Mia?! And now, now I have to do this. I have to punish you. It's the only way."

"Gorman, don't you fucking do it! I will kill you on the spot," Jackson swears.

"Kill me? I'm not gonna be around, Jackson. Mia and I will be together whether she likes it or not. I wanted us to get a house, be a family, but she messed that up. And now, if we can't live together, we will die together."

Pictures flash in my head—pictures of my son, his high school graduation, his first date, and all the birthdays that I will miss. The terror surging through me takes a back seat to my sudden wave of determination. There's no way I'm leaving my kid. There's no way I am going to let this crazy fucker be the end of me. All Jackson needs is space between Gorman and me; I know I have to find a way to make that happen.

"Before we jump, Gorman, can I please have one request?" I beg.

"No! You don't deserve it."

"I know I don't. I hurt you. You were good to me, you loved me, and I didn't get that. I'm sorry. You put up with my disobedience, so I know you're merciful and kind. Please be kind right now, and let me have my last request."

"What is it? What do you want?" he rages.

"You."

"What?" he asks, taken off guard.

"I tried to run away from you not because I was scared of you, but because I was scared of how much I love you. I've never felt love like the love I have for you. But I'm ready to face that love. I'm ready to be the woman you need."

"Liar! You're just trying to get out of this. It's not gonna happen. I'll kill you first," he bitterly announces.

"She's not lying. She wants you. That's why I haven't asked her to marry me; she's too into you to really commit to me. She wants you. And you can have her—alive."

I reach my hand above my head and gently brush his cheek. He sighs as my hand makes contact.

"Mark, please, baby. Forgive me. Let us be together, the way we were meant to be." He starts to loosen his hold on my neck, but his gun remains at my temple. I look up at him, reach out, and kiss his cheek; when my lips make contact, he drops his guard for a second. I elbow him hard in the gut and break away from his hold.

"You bitch!" Gorman cries out.

"Mia, down!" As the words fly out of Jackson's mouth, I hit the floor, and bullets ring out all around me. I look up, just in time to see Gorman fire several shots and then run up to the roof. Jackson looks back at me, and I signal that I'm okay. He takes off to the roof after Gorman. I follow them at a distance. Gorman fires yet another round at Jackson, but this time, one of the bullets lands.

"No!" I scream as the force of the bullet propels Jackson down to the ground. He's been shot in the chest. He's not moving. I rush to his side and cry hysterically. Gorman drags me kicking and screaming to the edge of the roof. He kicks me while I'm on the ground and tells me I don't deserve his love. I see movement from the corner of my eye. Jackson.

Gorman stands over me screaming, "You see, he couldn't protect you. He couldn't save you. I'm the one you need. I am your destiny! And you will always belong to—" Three shots ring out and hit Gorman in the chest. He tumbles backward and falls off the side of the building. Gorman's body hits the ground, and his head shatters on impact; splat! Gorman is dead.

Peace. Peace at last.

I crawl over to Jackson, who's groaning on the floor. I take off my jacket and use it to apply pressure on his wound.

"Babe, hold on, help is coming," I plead. He whispers something. I can't hear. I get closer to him.

"What is it, Jackson? What are you trying to say?"

"Do you think this will get me out of the bachelor auction?"

I wanted Jackson to stay in the hospital a little longer, but he didn't want to miss Argo's nursing school graduation. And the doctor said as long as he didn't overdo it, he should be okay. His fractured rib is healing nicely. His brothers teased and said he was only supposed to call on them if every rib was broken.

When we get to Argo's ceremony, we find Shelby is already there. I tell her to thank her husband for making a call on my behalf.

"Anytime, Mona Lisa." She smiles.

Sitting next to Shelby is Argo's dad. Thankfully, Gorman didn't seriously wound my best friend. I know that because when he gets on the stage to accept his certificate, he takes the time to pop his hips and blow kisses to us. Aaron and I laugh as we stand up and cheer for him. In fact, his dad, Jackson, and Shelby all stand up too. My best friend is a nurse, and I'm so damn proud of him.

When the ceremony is over, we go to Mrs. Hunter's house. Shelby introduced them, and they've been thick as thieves ever since. In fact, he's in her book club. Guess I know what that means…

Everyone is mingling in the garden, where the wait staff serve tray after tray of food. It's a beautiful night in Mrs. Hunter's garden, and everyone is having a blast, including the five brothers.

But then suddenly the music dies down, and everyone is quiet. I look around, not sure what's going on. "Hey, what's happening?" I ask. Aaron starts to giggle. And Argo begins to cry. I turn around and follow everyone's gaze—they are looking at Jackson getting on one knee.

"Mia Avery, there's something I've been meaning to ask you."

Epilogue

My stepson is giving a tour of his favorite aquarium. He's growing frustrated that his audience isn't receptive.

"Mom! Make her pay attention," Aaron says.

"Honey, she's five months old. I think she'd rather her older brother play with her," my wife suggests. Aaron rolls his eyes and stoops down to the baby stroller. He makes goofy faces, and sure enough, Melody gets really happy and bounces her body up and down. As soon as Aaron sees her getting excited, he does even sillier faces. She has my dark eyes and her mom's red hair. She's perfect.

I can't help but think about the first time we came here. I never thought my life would turn out like this, and every day I'm grateful. In addition to the birth of my daughter, I married the love of my life, and Aaron calls me Dad. In the beginning, Tom had an issue with it, and that made Aaron feel guilty. Mia worried about it, and I promised her that I would handle it.

When Tom got back from London, I had him over for a beer and explained that I would never want to take his place. I told him I'm good being the "additional" dad, and that Aaron wanted nothing more than to see us get along. It took some doing, but now we're on the same page. When Tom takes Aaron out, they have a good time. But we always keep Tom's visits as a surprise rather than an expectation. And to be honest, he's gotten better at showing up for Aaron. That has meant the world to Mia.

"Are we ready to go?" Aaron asks.

"Okay, let's go," his mom says. Normally, Aaron could stay here all day, but he's spending the afternoon with Wyatt's boys, and he can't wait. It's the perfect time to go since Melody needs to take her nap soon.

When we get back to the house, I find Endless in the living room, and once again I have to take our keys from her. This is the third time.

"Seriously, how does she get her hands on our keys?" I ask Mia.

"She's Shelby," Mia says as she shrugs her shoulders.

"Don't you have a home?" I ask her.

"Rude. Very rude. But I forgive you because Argo and I are headed for yoga. And you will not stop my chi," Shelby says.

"Speaking of Argo, how did his dad take meeting his new boyfriend?" I ask.

"It went really well—too well. Now Argo's dad tags him in all these posts on Facebook having to do with adoption. I think he's ready to be a grandfather," Mia says.

"His father is relentless. That's why I'm taking him to the spa after yoga. Soak up the stress," Endless says.

"He'll love that. Just remind him he's got babysitting duties tomorrow—date night," Mia says.

"Where are you two going?" Endless asks me.

"There's a new hot wing flavor at the bar by the office. It's called Blue Flames, and we have a bet going that I can eat more of them than he can," Mia says as she tends to the baby.

"Ha! You're going down, Dr. Hunter," I reply as I grab Mia's ass and pull her in for a kiss. It takes so little for her to get me turned on, She looks into my eyes and right away, I know we are on the same page.

"Um, Endless, watch the kids for a few minutes. We'll be right back!" I say as I take Mia by her hand and run upstairs.

Endless shouts up to us, "Stay away from the coat closet. I hung up my jacket in there. Hey, I mean it; respect the Armani!"

END OF BOOK 4

Author's Note

If you enjoyed this book, please take a moment to leave a review on the site where you bought this book.

Join us for book 5: *Anything for Family* (The story of Gage Hunter, pre order now!)

Also please stop by our Facebook page, like us:

https://www.facebook.com/lolastvilromance

And sign up for our mailing list so you'll be the first to know when our next romance book comes out!

http://eepurl.com/c-gh7T